CITY COUSIN

AND OTHER STORIES

*T*his is a collection of eight short stories about life in China today. The authors describe in glowing terms and from different angles new people that have stepped forth, and new and remarkable events that have occurred throughout the country. In these stories the reader meets a store-keeper in a mountain area who gives her whole heart to serving the peasants, People's Liberation Army men who guard the land and cherish the people. There are also a Party branch secretary who leads fisherfolk to transform their hamlet, a young docker growing in maturity, and young people who go to the countryside from school with lofty aims to build a new village.

These stories, most of them written by amateurs, are near enough to life to afford the reader to share in the thoughts of the characters.

HARVARD–YENCHING
LIBRARY

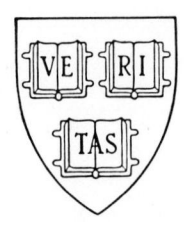

HARVARD UNIVERSITY
LIBRARY

CITY COUSIN

AND OTHER STORIES

FOREIGN LANGUAGES PRESS ∗ PEKING ∗ 1973

PL 2658 .E8 C58 1973x

City cousin, and other stories

Printed in the People's Republic of China

Contents

CITY COUSIN *Sha Ping-teh*	1
LOOK FAR, FLY FAR *Shanghai dockers' spare-time writing group*	19
THE CALL *Chu Yu-tung*	38
SPRING COMES TO A FISHING VILLAGE *Hung Shan*	52
THE FERRY AT BILLOWS HARBOUR *Fang Nan*	66
A SHOULDER POLE *Yueh Chang-kuei*	87
WHEN THE PERSIMMONS RIPENED *Ko Niu*	100
HOME LEAVE *Hsueh Chiang*	116

City Cousin

Sha Ping-teh

A new moon hung over the rooftops as several girls, returning home at sunset, called to each other to go to Maoya's house.

Merry, yet serious, they were a noisy band of middle-school graduates. "Why don't you come out and see us, Maoya?" came one insistent voice.

"Is she putting on airs now that she's become an old hand?" came another voice, quite shrill. This happy and excited group flocked around another girl who was in the courtyard.

The girl was Maoya. After graduating from the primary school in town she hadn't gone to the county middle school as most of her friends had, but had come back home to the farm. Maoya had proved to be not only a skilled farmer but was known in the village as being fond of talking and laughing.

She could out-talk many a young man. But now she was mute, unable to hold her own against these friends of hers since childhood.

Then the eldest of the girls, who seemed to be their spokesman, asked for quiet, suppressed her own smile and declared in all seriousness: "Maoya, we've come home to work on the farm. We were talking about it on the train and thought we should organize a 'girls team.' We want you as team leader, to help us — teach us to do farm work, so that we too can help build our socialist new countryside!"

"You'll do that, won't you?" injected a girl who wore her short braids standing almost upright.

"For goodness' sake, is *that* all?" Maoya broke the solemnity with her laughter. "That's not so difficult."

"So you agree?" the girls pressed.

"I agree . . . . I agree to recommend someone to you."

"Ah, foxy, aren't you!" the girls shouted.

"You're the best farmer of all us village girls. Don't think we don't know!" the girl with the braids countered with a show of belligerence.

"My dear little bureaucrats," Maoya retorted, evading the threat, "that may have been true in the past. Now, there's a girl here who's a better farmer than I."

"Who is it?"

"Lien."

"Oh," the girls could only say, and looked at each other.

"It's not surprising that you don't know," Maoya explained, "because you've been away. Sit down, girls, and I'll tell you how it is."

The girls dropped onto anything in the courtyard that could serve as seats and waited for Maoya to begin.

*

My cousin Lien hadn't given me a very good impression at our first meeting.

One summer day at noon, when I came home from the fields, I found a girl in the kitchen helping my mother get the meal. I leaned my hoe against the wall just inside the gate and called:

"Who's the guest, ma?"

My mother looked up from the wheat-cakes she was rolling. "When will you ever learn manners?" she said reprovingly. "Why, this is your cousin from the city."

I had heard that I had a cousin in the city, and that she was two years older than I, also that her name was Lien. Come to think of it, she should have finished senior middle school by now. I had never been to the city where she lived — it was in another county — and she hadn't come to visit us either, so we had never met. Now here she was at last. I began to size up this cousin of mine.

Lien was an attractive girl, slim, of medium height, and with a fresh, clear complexion. She smiled as she came out to greet me, two long braids of fine hair reaching to her waist. She asked in a gentle voice:

"Just come off shift, cousin?"

"Come off shift!" — now there was a city dweller for you. The soft, intellectual type really made me squirm, but since it was a cousin I was meeting for the first time, I had to be polite.

At lunch I asked her: "What do you think of our Chiangchun Village, cousin?"

She smiled. "Very nice."

My mother stopped my next question. "That girl is forever boasting about our village," she told Lien. Then to me she said: "Lien is going to live here and work in our team. She'll know soon enough what our village is like. Now eat your lunch."

"Honest? Is that right?"

"Yes, cousin." Lien stopped plying her chopsticks and nodded. "I finished senior middle school, but I didn't try for college. I thought I ought to work for a year in the country first."

Lien obviously meant it, and my mother was serious too. I took another look at my city cousin. A slip of a girl like her. A couple of days in the village might be all right, but to "work for a year!"

That afternoon, when Lien said she'd work with me in the fields, my mother wasn't sure.

"What's the hurry, Lien? You've just come. We'll have a long chat here at home."

"Won't we have lots of time for chats later on, aunt?"

"You've come all this distance. You ought to rest."

"Why should I, if I'm not tired? When I am, I'll rest even without you telling me."

We were right in the middle of hoeing around the bean shoots. We girls were competing with the boys. What time was there for chatting? Without a word, I got another hoe out of the shed and took Lien off with me to the bean field.

Did you ever see anybody learning to hoe? It's really a sight. Actually, there isn't anything so hard about it, but Lien was more excited than a kid on her first day at school. It was as if she were starting a brand new life. Watching her with that hoe, I didn't know whether to laugh or cry. She swung the light little blade as if it weighed a ton, and it just wouldn't land where she aimed it. She hacked wildly for some time, knocking down bean shoots left and right, while the weeds remained standing. The poor girl didn't know where to put her feet. When she stood close, she couldn't swing the hoe; when she stepped back, she trampled the plants in the row behind.

"Why torture yourself, cousin?" I said. "Go take a rest under that tree."

Lien gave me a startled glance, then her face reddened. She turned and gazed at the patch she had just hoed. It looked as if the hens had been at it. Her smile was positively pathetic. But she got hold of herself, wiped some of the sweat from her forehead, bit her lower lip, and went on hoeing.

After work, she walked home close to me. "What's the knack to this hoeing, cousin?" she asked.

We had beaten the boys that day, and I was feeling fine. I was much too absorbed, talking gaily with the other girls, to go into such questions. "I'll show you tomorrow," I put her off.

Either I wasn't a good teacher, or she wasn't a good pupil, for after the whole morning's teaching she was still as bad as the day before. Word reached us: "The boys have caught up." I was very irritated, and stopped bothering with her.

At noon, when we came home for lunch, our team leader Uncle Cheng-kang sent for me. In a serious voice, he said: "Lien has just come from the city. We must take pains to help her."

"I wasted a whole morning," I said, "and the boys caught up with us. They wouldn't have if I wasn't trying to help her. It's not my fault she can't learn."

"You've got to be patient," he said. "Lien's come to our village for training in answer to Chairman Mao's call, and that's taking a big step forward, isn't it? We poor and lower-middle peasants ought to help her willingly."

It was too hot to go back to the fields right after lunch, and the girls called for me to go with them and enjoy the cool under the willows south of the village. As I was going out the gate I remembered

Lien, and I shouted for her, but there was no answer. I looked in the house. She wasn't there.

"Where's Lien, ma?" I asked.

My mother looked up from washing dishes. "She was here a minute ago," she said.

That's funny, I thought. I noticed a small red-covered notebook open on the table. Lien had been writing in it for a long time before going to bed the previous night. Had she been writing again? There, on the first page in large characters was the sentence: "May you strike deep roots in our vast countryside and mature quickly."

It must be a diary she was keeping! Lien was probably very unhappy. I hadn't been very kind to her the past two days. The first time she'd ever been away from home, and she'd travelled quite a distance to come to our village, and I . . . . Why, she must be miserable. I got very upset.

"Isn't Lien around?" my mother asked.

I mumbled something, then dashed out. Peasants I asked on the road said they'd seen Lien leave the village going west. Probably looking for a quiet place for a good cry, I was really worried at the thought.

I looked for her everywhere — in the gully, the grove . . . , but she was nowhere to be found. I felt very sorry, standing there. Then, I happened to look off towards the bean field. Two people were there in the patch we'd hoed that morning, and one of them was Lien. I cut straight across the fields towards her, relieved.

Uncle Chen-kuei, the secretary of our Communist Party branch, was teaching her to hoe. He was very patient, and she was very attentive. I halted a good distance off, too embarrassed to hail them.

Lien turned around and smiled when she saw me. "So it's you, Maoya," she called.

She said it with such affection that it seemed she wasn't angry with me after all. I bounded forward and flung my arms around her neck.

It was a scorching hot day and the fields were like a steamer. Lien's face was as red as a boiled prawn; sweat poured off her. I grabbed her hoe.

"Let's go home, Lien," I urged, "I'll help you tomorrow." "It's too hot today."

But Lien refused to let go of the hoe. To the old Party secretary she said with a smile: "You go back with her, uncle. I know you're busy. I'll practise here by myself."

Uncle Chen-kuei agreed we should knock off. "Why not go home and cool off, Lien?" he suggested. "You can't swallow a whole meal down in one gulp."

"Are you out of your mind, Lien?" That was my mother, who had come to find us. "Let me see your hands," she ordered.

Lien put out her hands, palms up. They were red and blistered. One of the blisters had broken.

"It takes time to learn farming, child," my mother said reprovingly. "You're not supposed just to charge into it."

Uncle Chen-kuei added gently, "Go and rest, Lien. This won't do."

"But I've come here for training, and I mustn't be afraid of these things," she said, shooting a contemptuous glance first at her blisters and then at the scorching sun.

With that she turned to proceed with the hoeing....

That night I happened to wake. It was very late, but Lien was still not asleep. She was lying on her back, her sore hands, which my mother had bandaged, folded over her chest and her dark eyes fixed on the ceiling. I called to her softly.

"Oh, you're awake too," she said. She sat up and smoothed her hair. "I've been thinking and thinking," she said in a low voice. "I just can't settle down."

"Don't worry, Lien," I comforted her. "You've only just come."

"I know," she replied. "But I've learned a lot here. While Uncle Chen-kuei was teaching me to hoe this noon, he told me of his childhood, when he was hired by the landlord to labour. Those scars on his back! He told me something of the bitter life of the poor and lower-middle peasants in the village under the landlord's cruel oppression and exploitation. It made my heart ache. I've been thinking how much class exploitation our elders suffered. They shed their blood and gave their lives in order to restore the state power back into the hands of the people; now it's up to us younger generation to build our motherland well. How can I yield to hardship and quit just because learning's difficult? No. I cannot forget the Party's expectations and trust in us."

The moonlight pouring through the window shone on her proud, stubborn head. I was suddenly aware of the strong will that burned within Lien's slight frame.

With her determination, Lien learned to hoe that summer, and to reap and plough that autumn. She was like a locomotive with a full head of steam. Day or night, rain or shine, she kept on.

At the time, it seemed to me she was over-doing things. When the autumn sowing began, she asked me to teach her how to use the seeder! That's one of the trickiest and most tiring jobs in farming. None of us girls knew how.

"The boys in our team can manage," I said. "Why should we learn?"

Lien looked a little annoyed. "A peasant ought to be able to do everything in farming, and do it well."

"But that's the most complicated job of all," I explained.

"That's exactly why we should learn," she insisted. "Later on, our team will have a tractor, then a combine. They're even more complicated. Does that mean we girls aren't going to drive them?"

All right, I thought, you go ahead and learn. I went to the people in charge of the animals and equipment and talked them into lending me what I wanted. I returned leading an ox, with the seeder on my shoulder and a basket of wheat seed in my hand.

Lien was delighted. She rolled up her sleeves excitedly and we went to a field north of the village that was ready for sowing. With me leading the ox and Lien handling the seeder, we set to work.

But we had no sooner started than our troubles began. If we rocked the seeder too gently the seed didn't fall through. If we shook it too violently it scattered wide of the furrow. If the ox plodded too slowly the planting was too dense. If the ox was too fast the guide-shares popped out.

Lien, in her excitement, pressed down too hard and one of the guide-shares hit a rock. There was a sharp crack as the metal tip snapped off.

I pulled the ox to a halt. "I told you we couldn't do it," I cried, "but you had to show off."

I peered back at the three crooked rows we had just seeded. I was upset, but Lien was paralysed. She stared, dumb-founded, at the broken guide-share. I didn't have the heart to say more.

"We've got lots of extra guide-shares," I consoled, pretending a calm I didn't feel. "It's nothing to worry about."

As luck would have it, Uncle Cheng-kang happened to pass our field on his way back from a meeting. He saw our crooked furrows and came running towards us, shouting: "Goodness me, is that any way to seed?" But when he saw the broken share tip, he was really angry. "You girls are mad," he fumed.

"Learning to use the seeder is all right, but you ought to get someone to teach you."

Lien was scared. I looked at Uncle Cheng-kang. "What are you getting excited about?" I asked. "It's only a guide-share. We've got plenty in the store-room."

"Generous, aren't you," he bellowed. "You're really generous. Of course our team's got spares. But how long would they last if everyone acted like you girls?"

Still shouting, he led off the ox, carrying the seeder and the basket of seed.

In the afternoon, he sent someone to teach Lien how to use the seeder. Lien finally learned, and it was really she who encouraged the rest of us to learn.

More and more of our commune members got to like Lien. They said she had spunk. Some people even said that she was the best farmer of all the girls in the village.

Naturally, I was glad that Lien was learning fast. But to claim that she was such a good farmer — I certainly couldn't accept that.

When the ploughing started last spring, I got up especially early the first day and picked myself a first-rate ox from the barn and a good plough from the store-room, and went off with the others to the fields. I was in high spirits.

How clear the sky is in early spring, how warm the sun! The soft breezes, the voices singing — it really makes you feel wonderful. After the plots to be ploughed were assigned and we hitched up our oxen, I called out:

"Hey, comrades, let's have a competition and see who's the best farmer."

Lien nodded at me and smiled. She knew I had her in mind, but she seemed pleased nonetheless.

"Right," she shouted. "Whoever ploughs the best gets a prize."

Whips cracked, and over a dozen ploughs set out. I glanced at Lien. A whip in one hand and the other guiding the plough, she advanced proudly. Clumps of earth rose on one side of her plough share and arranged themselves in a neat row. Ploughing the length of the field five times up and back, Lien left the other girls far behind.

I couldn't pass her no matter how I tried, and I was very upset. I was born on a farm, and had been doing this work for many more years than she. Why was I behind? I simply had to pass her, or the reputation I had earned in the past two years would be ruined. I began leaving wider and wider spaces between my furrows.

When I had made three or four trips, Lien walked over to me.

"What in the world are you doing?" she demanded.

I halted my ox. "What's wrong?"

"You don't know!" She pointed indignantly at my patch. "Call that ploughing?"

I looked. I had left huge spaces between my rows. My face burned. "I won't do it any more," I mumbled.

"Never mind," she snapped. "Let's put a few more furrows in those gaps. We'll do it together."

Lien led her ox to my plot and ploughed side by side with me. "Yes," she sighed, "you too have this problem."

"What problem?" I asked.

"The problem of class stand, viewpoint and feelings," said she. "A person who is merely good at hoeing, ploughing, harrowing and harvesting isn't necessarily a good farmer. The important thing is to learn from the poor and lower-middle peasants their class stand, viewpoint and feelings. Remember that day when Uncle Cheng-kang saw the seeds wasted and the broken guide-share, he got angry with us. But we were quite indifferent. Again, one day on our way to the fields we saw some cow dung on the road, but we just passed it by. When Uncle Chen-kuei saw it he shovelled it onto the fields. Such things seem trifling, but they show that the poor and lower-middle peasants do not work for personal fame or gain. What do you think?"

I flushed. How right Lien was. Why are the uncles Chen-kuei and Cheng-kang always conscientious and earnest in everything they do? It's simply because they work for the collective, for socialism.

Lien had changed. Not only had her fine long braids been snipped off, but her fair face had filled out and toughened. Even her temperament had changed too. You could hear her hearty laugh all over the village now. She sang in the fields. Wherever girls or women gathered, there was Lien, one among them. During work breaks the old men were always asking her to read to them from Chairman Mao's works, or else the newspaper. Lien never seemed to rest. She was like a ball of fire, bringing warmth and excitement everywhere she went.

One evening I went with her to the stream south of the village to sharpen some sickles. Silvery moonlight coated the gurgling water. The fragrance of fresh grain drifted to us on the breeze from the fields. I sat down on a stone slab and dangled my feet in the stream. There was Lien whetting a blade. Her year was nearly up, and she should be leaving. I liked her enormously and didn't like to think of her going.

Several of the sickles in my hand splashed into the water.

"What makes you so absent-minded tonight?" Lien asked.

I felt my nose tingling. There was no use trying to hide it from her. I told her what was troubling me.

She laughed. "You certainly have a good memory. Why, I've forgotten all about college entrance exams!"

"You mean you're not going?"

She cocked her head sideways, still rubbing her blade, and looked at me. "You'd like me to stay?"

"Of course I would!"

"I feel," she said, "that going to the countryside at the Party's call is only the first step for educated youth. But can they strike roots in the countryside? Will they really qualify as peasants? That's the test."

I decided to sound her out further. "Of course, we're not so well off here as people in the cities," I said.

"It's true, our cities are fine," replied Lien. "But our generation is responsible for the countryside as well. It's up to us to speed development in the countryside — mechanization, electrification. It's up to us to help close the gap between town and country."

*

The moon had climbed higher now, and the village was quiet. Especially quiet was the small courtyard where the girls sat.

"Girls," began Maoya, "what do you think of my recommendation for team leader?"

Replying with another question, they inquired, "Where's Lien?"

"After work this afternoon she went to a brigade meeting," Maoya said. "She's a member of our Youth League general branch committee now, in charge of propaganda work."

"Will she be back tonight?"

"Of course."

The girls began to whisper among themselves.

June was a busy month on the farm. Maoya was awakened by Lien at daybreak and, taking up her hoe, silently followed the girl out. She was thinking about what the girls had decided the night before. When they reached the big gingko tree, suddenly over a dozen girls rushed out and surrounded Maoya and Lien, declaring in chorus:

"We've formed a farm girls' team and want Lien to head it!"

Lien stepped back, at a loss until she guessed what had happened. Then she smoothed back a wisp of her hair, a smile playing on her face. The girls took a step back too, wondering what she had in mind.

"Well, if you really mean to make me your team leader, girls, I give you fair warning," she said.

"Why?"

"Do you think you can stand my orders?"

"So long as they help us to build our socialist countryside, we'll welcome your orders," the girls answered.

"All right then, let's start now." The new team leader nodded her approval. "Hoes up. March to the fields!" directed Lien with a wave of her hand.

Through the cool morning dew, now glistening in the sun, the girls walked briskly to the fields, to the lush, fragrant fields. . . .

Illustrated by Tsai Jung

Look Far, Fly Far

Shanghai dockers'
spare-time writing group

Fang Hsiao, a girl of medium height, ruddy-faced, her short hair tied in a knot, walked along vigorously in her father's faded army coat, her big eyes flashing. She stopped in front of the post office, pulled out a letter, contemplated it for a moment, then said to herself, "To Fang Chien-ming, *S.S. Chang Feng*, c/o Oversea Shipping Company. All correct." She slipped it into the mailbox, and smiled. "Dad will be very pleased to know that I'm going to be one of the first women crane operators." And she was going to the job on an ocean-going ship right away. The thought infused new strength in her. She quickened her steps. Her destination was Shanghai's Red Flag Wharf where the ship was moored.

*

What made Hsiao become a crane operator? The story has to be told from the beginning.

Hsiao first came to work on the dock with her schoolmates last autumn, a busy season for both the peasants and dockers. The moment she stepped on the wharf she was struck by a huge slogan in red: "Fight for three months to overfulfil the yearly target ahead of schedule!"

Battery-powered lift trucks laden with cargo shuttled to and fro. Cranes turned their arms in all directions. The hustle and bustle made an indelible impression on Hsiao and her schoolmates. They realized that this was a battlefield, a frontline.

Very active by nature, Hsiao was immediately astir. Taking the dockers unawares, she climbed into the cab of No. 308 crane. She fingered the switch. Crash! The thunderous noise scared her out of her wits. She slipped down without being observed and hid in a corner. A crane operator helping longshoremen unload rice in a barge jumped quickly ashore. After having inspected the crane, he was confused that no one was about. He took off his cap and fanned himself with it, the cowlick on his forehead fluttering.

"A woman!" Hsiao exclaimed.

Not till this moment did the woman crane operator Yeh Chih-ying see her. She and Hsiao soon became friends.

They often met by the Huangpu dock side, chatting to their hearts' content, their eyes fastened on the river and the hovering sea-gulls.

Like a sister Chih-ying told her a lot of new things. Cranes, for instance, were of different types and powered differently. No. 308, for example, was run by electricity. Nowadays women not only operated cranes, but loaded and unloaded cargo as well. "We women are half the population, you know." And they burst out laughing. But how was it that they did not teach girls in the past to work on the cranes? Chih-ying told her that there was such a plan, but under the influence of Liu Shao-chi's revisionist line, it never materialized. Of course that was before the Cultural Revolution.

Hsiao was firmly convinced that women could do just as well as men and that one day there would be as many women as men working on the cranes.

Not long after Hsiao told her father that she wanted to be a crane operator, he wrote: "Revolutionary work may be varied, but the goal is the same: to realize communist ideals. You ought to plunge into the revolutionary movement and integrate yourself with the workers and peasants, learn from them so as to be re-educated by them and have your ideology remoulded. You mustn't choose your work merely from personal interest."

Her father urged her to study Chairman Mao's works on how to serve the people. Hsiao had great respect for her father, a Communist who had been decorated several times during the war and who stood on the side of Chairman Mao's revolutionary line during the Cultural Revolution. Now he worked as a political commissar on *S.S. Chang Feng*.

Although she felt that her father was right, she could not help thinking that he did not understand her. It was not merely personal interest that made her want to be a crane operator. She wanted to prove that women were just as capable as men. In any case she must join the ranks of workers, by whom she would have herself re-educated ideologically.

Together with other young folk, Hsiao developed like a good seed set in fertile soil, sprouting and growing into a sturdy plant within the short space of one year.

The Party branch secretary Wu and Communist worker Yeh, Chih-ying's father, all paid particular attention to this. They discussed the matter in the Party committee and decided to give Yeh the task of training the girl as a crane operator.

When Wu told her this decision, Hsiao was pleased at first, but soon she became pensive. The Party secretary found from the expression on her bronzed face that she was no longer the childish girl she had been a year before. Her sharp flashing eyes concentrated all the resoluteness and solemnity of her personality. Finally it came out that her father's advice had much to do with the shaping of her thought.

"What your father told you is right," Wu told her. "You can't do a revolutionary job merely from personal interest, and trying to prove that women are just as capable as men isn't correct either. We are marching towards the great goal of communism. What we ought to do is to bring credit to our socialist motherland."

Hsiao nodded. The Party secretary's words opened a new vista for her and new strength flowed in her. She wrote to her father the moment she came home, telling him how she longed to have *S.S. Chang Feng* dock the very next day so that he could see her operating a crane on board.

*

After mailing the letter Hsiao threaded her way quickly through the wharf. Her heart thumped with excitement as she stepped on board *S.S. Combat* with Yeh and went towards the cranes.

But it was the most awkward day in her life. Yeh was loading the ship. How dexterously he lifted the cargo clear of the wharf and lowered it neatly into the hold! But she could only bungle. A bale of cotton turned a somersault and slipped onto the deck with a thud. It was Yeh who put it into the net again. She bit her lips, ashamed of herself.

"Never mind," Yeh said. "Take a rest before you operate the machine again."

The kind words stung her much more painfully than scolding.

Lashed by a strong wind, the river began to heave. A flock of sea-gulls, braving the head wind, headed off in the distance, their wings outstretched.

Yeh took Hsiao by the hand and, pointing to the vanishing birds, said meaningfully, "Only in a head wind can you exercise your wings." He tapped Hsiao's shoulder for emphasis and went on, pronouncing each word slowly, "We must advance in face of difficulties. This is the way revolutionary work is done."

With fresh courage Hsiao climbed into the cab and resumed her work. The wind abated into a light breeze as the evening set in. There was a lot of hustle and bustle on the brightly lit wharf. As her crane came around, Hsiao's nerves tightened. Sweat glittered on the tip of her nose, and her breath came hard. But Yeh directing the operation from below reassured her from time to time with encouraging glances.

Beginning the next day one could often see a girl in a red sweater doing gymnastics on the parallel bars east of the basketball court, perspiring in spite of the cutting north wind. Hsiao was trying to build strength in her arms.

Judging by their appearance, Yeh, now approaching fifty, was a serious veteran worker while Hsiao, not quite twenty, was a lively girl. But they got along very well together. They did not speak much, but they studied together, thought the same way and worked as one person. Yeh's spirit of serving the people wholly and entirely seeped deep into Hsiao's mind. Unconsciously, Hsiao assimilated Yeh's ways. Whenever she saw a piece of cargo tilted on a flat car, she would put it right. She would pick up pieces of cast-off rope and keep it for future use. She even took on Yeh's habit of throwing his padded jacket casually over his shoulders.

As for the veteran worker, whenever Hsiao was mentioned, he would say in his Shantung accent, "Ah, my Little Hsiao," as though she were his own daughter.

*

One morning, after a night of drizzle, the weeping willow buds sprouted. Washed by the rain, the air smelt fresh and clean. The holly on both sides of the road leading to the wharf looked green and thriving. Hsiao felt equally fresh and buoyant. *S.S. Chang Feng* had just docked after a long voyage. She had not seen her father for half a year. But what cheered her most was the assignment given her by Yeh to operate the crane on this ocean-going ship made by China herself!

Hsiao flushed with excitement, her heart almost jumping into her mouth. Yeh, however, frowned. "The *Chang Feng* has very big cargo hatches," he said. "You can be bold. But mind you, work with great concentration."

Acknowledging the advice with a "Yes," Hsiao proudly climbed into the operator's cab. She took a long breath to calm herself, then began to work. Huge aluminium slabs were lifted slowly out of the hold, moved over the deck and, guided by Yeh's signals, lowered exactly into the waiting truck on the wharf.

Hsiao heard someone say, "When we sailed on our last voyage, we didn't have any woman crane operator. Now half a year later we have a skilled one."

"She's excellent" another added.

"I understand that our Political Commissar Fang's daughter is also a crane operator."

"You're always on the scent of everything, and this time you're right," said the dispatcher, but his voice was very low.

Hsiao's heart beat fast. She looked around. The wheel house was empty. Her eyes went back to Yeh and his signals. "We were hit by a hurricane on our voyage, but Political Commissar Fang kept calm throughout . . . ," someone was commenting. "A heavy wave rose like a mountain, then it split, leaving a hole deep enough to swamp everything. . . . Comrades were confident . . . peril. . . . The *Chang Feng* rode it out . . . steaming ahead. . . . "

Hsiao's heart was as stirred as the person describing the storming voyage. Her gaze turned again to the wheel house and she seemed to see her father there encouraging the crew.

"Stop! Stop!"

Hsiao frantically pushed the switch to "stop" but it was too late. She heard a crash like a landslide on the wharf. She jumped out of the cab, crossed the deck and looked over the railing. Two tons of aluminium slabs were dumped on the wharf in a shapeless heap. A young docker below growled, "What a crane operator! Doesn't know when to stop it? Look what a mess she has made! Now we have to straighten it out. What a waste of time!"

Hsiao was stunned as though she had been beaten on the head by a club.

"Fang Hsiao!" A grave voice. Yeh, face set, was looking at her. "Why didn't you listen to the command? Imagine what would have happened if there were people under your crane!" The veteran paused and then said, "You're controlling not only the movement of a crane but the property of the people."

It was the first time she had seen Yeh so upset. She wanted to explain but words failed her. Just then her father appeared on deck and walked over to her. Yeh, his face still set, was issuing her an order, "Stay away and think it over!"

"Stop working?" She felt as though icy water had been poured over her head. She was even more flustered that her father was standing behind her. Now the icy water turned hot and her face flushed crimson.

She walked towards the dining room, head hanging, lips pursed. She was angry with herself. The noise from the dining room came into her ears. She halted at the door, reluctant to go in. Taking her completely unawares two hands suddenly covered her eyes from behind. It must be Chih-ying, who was always playing pranks. "Away with you!" she said petulantly and wrested herself out of her clasp.

"Angry, eh? Who's offended you?" Chih-ying asked in a deliberately irritating voice.

"No one. I myself am to blame."

"You're the offender?" Chih-ying took Hsiao by the arm and pulled her into the dining room. "Tell me frankly what's the matter," she said with concern.

Hsiao could no longer contain herself. Tears brimming in her eyes, she said, "Your father was angry with me. He doesn't want me to handle the crane. And father. . . ."

"My father or yours?" Chih-ying asked impatiently.

"Both. . . ." Hsiao took a deep breath.

"In that case," Chih-ying said, pretending a deep sigh, "both fathers are angry with you, criticized you and won't allow you to operate the machine." She emphasized "fathers" as though there were many fathers who had exerted pressure on her, looking so comical that Hsiao giggled.

"Little Hsiao," Chih-ying said, assuming a serious face, "think over carefully why they did not allow you to go on working."

Yeh suddenly appeared in front of them. He flung a glance at both of them, then turned and walked away.

In a flash he brought back several pieces of steamed bread and bowls of soup from the dining room. Handing Hsiao a piece of bread, Chih-ying said, "Time for lunch."

"When a child learns to walk," Yeh said in a soft voice, "it often stumbles and falls. What is to be done?"

"Get on its feet and try again," said Chih-ying.

"What do you say to that, Hsiao?" Yeh asked the pensive girl.

"Well...." Hsiao nodded.

"There's a saying among us crane operators," Yeh said, "that in order to be able to regulate the machine we must first regulate our thinking."

Thoughts crowded into Hsiao's mind as she walked back home. Why didn't Yeh allow me to operate the machine? Why did I let something distract me from doing the job? Yeh was right. In order to be able to regulate my machine I must first regulate my thinking.

In the evening Political Commissar Fang had a heart-to-heart talk with his daughter. His grey hair and the deep lines on his forehead brought out by the lamplight intensified a facial expression both serious and affectionate. "What kind of attitude do you think you should take towards a revolutionary job? Comrade Norman Bethune was very conscientious in doing his work, so are our veteran workers. But you?" The political commissar paused, then said in a clear, low voice, "Any slip in your work will inevitably bring loss to the state. On the battlefield defeat always comes in the wake of negligence. Carelessness is a kind of irresponsibility towards the revolution and the people."

A tremor went through Hsiao's whole being. "I was wrong," she said painfully. "I didn't put strict demands on myself."

The political commissar stood up and paced up and down the room. "You're like a young bird just trying your wings. The moment you can lift yourself up in the air, you forget everything. That's why you nearly dropped into the Huangpu River." This plunged Hsiao into meditation. The political commissar continued, "A colt has to gallop a lot on the prairie before he becomes a steed. Sea-gulls must exercise in storms before they can have strong wings. You'll never acquire skill without practice and trials. Yeh stopped you working for a time only to make you gallop faster and fly higher."

Hsiao mulled over these words.

"Tell me what you think," the political commissar broke the silence.

Hsiao's eyes suddenly sparkled. She reached for Chairman Mao's essay *In Memory of Norman Bethune* that lay on the table, and began to read. The political commissar smiled and left the room.

Time ticked away, second by second. Although it was late at night, Hsiao's room was still alight, and so was her face. She was deeply engrossed in studying and meditating on what Chairman Mao said in the essay.

In the notebook which she always kept handy she jotted down these lines: "I like to sing. But I'll sing out of tune if I don't go by the score. That's what happened to me today in my work. My thoughts went astray, hence the accident."

She stood up and looked around the room for things to practise manipulating a crane.

A knock on the door. Political Commissar Fang opened it. It was Yeh. "Where is our Hsiao?" he asked, warmly grasping the commissar's hand.

"In her room. Come with me." The political commissar led the way. At the door of his daughter's room, the commissar stopped short in surprise. A soap-dish loaded with buttons hung in the air suspended by two strings from a horizontal bar of the mosquito net frame on the bed. The girl was manipulating the soap-dish by pulling or paying out the strings.

Neither men spoke. Nor did Hsiao discover them, so absorbed was she in her practice. Yeh gently put an ash-tray where the soap-dish was to land. Only when the "cargo" was safely unloaded into the ash-tray did she notice the visitors.

"Oh, Yeh!" she exclaimed.

"Pay attention to your crane," Yeh exhorted.

"Yes," she said, quickly returning to her soap-dish.

This little scene made everything clear to the veteran docker. He had nothing to complain about in a girl who was so conscientious with her work. "You can work on the crane tomorrow, alone," he said.

Hsiao had not expected such a generous gesture. She gaped at Yeh — what a familiar and kind face! She recognized the scar on his forehead and the story behind it. It was where the foreman of the dock in the old days had hit him. He had led his fellow longshoremen in a bitter struggle against the bastard, who was so scared in the end that he never dared to touch the workers again. His bronzed face and the deep lines on his forehead were a record of decades of hard life on the dock, but the kind, contented smile came to him only after liberation — how much trust and encouragement it expressed!

"Comrade Wu, the Party secretary, also wanted to have a chat with you," he said to her. "But I told him it was not necessary. Good iron can stand all sorts of tempering and trials. You must be prepared to go through these too. How can you become fine steel otherwise?" He burst into hearty laughter.

A series of ideas flashed across her mind: control, aluminium slabs, ash-tray, independent operation. . . . She realized that Yeh had been trying to teach her to fly like a sea-gull, with her wings outstretched, through the storms towards the sun.

*

The huge ship towered alongside the third berth. The words *Chang Feng* stood out boldly on the bow setting off her august stature all the more. Now thoroughly cleaned, the ship looked more majestic and ready any time to set sail for another long voyage.

Crate after crate of cargo were being lowered into her hold. As the weight increased the ship settled deeper into the water, with her bow a bit raised. The sun beat down, shafts dancing on her well-polished railings.

An hour before she took over her shift, Hsiao received instructions from Party Secretary Wu in the dispatcher's room. "In the cargo there is one piece weighing seven tons," he said. "But our cranes can lift only three and half tons at a time. So we've commissioned a floating crane, *S.S. Sunlight*, for the purpose. It will arrive at 4:30 p.m. Can you manage that?"

"Certainly," Hsiao said with confidence, her eyes shining with determination. Then she made for the door.

"Wait a minute!" The Party secretary stopped her. "You know, this is an assignment from Yeh, who told me yesterday that you can certainly handle the job."

"Yeh. . . ." A flood of warmth rushed through her being and her eyes became moist. Grasping the secretary's hands, she said, "Party Secretary Wu, I can only prove it to you by doing it."

Hsiao stepped onto *S.S. Chang Feng* with big strides. She planted the red flag which she had brought with her on top of the second cargo hatch so that she could recognize it while working. Then she climbed into the cab of her crane.

She switched on the machine. The crane began to move. The hook went up and down obediently as she willed it. The cargo crates were deposited in neat piles in the hold. Because the workers of the first shift had overfulfilled their target, the seven-ton piece had to be loaded at 3 p.m. But the floating crane would not arrive until four. To the dockers every minute counted.

Party Secretary Wu and Dispatcher Kao gathered the men together to try to find a way out. It was common sense that a crane could never lift twice what it was built for. True, there was a special device on the ship kept in reserve for raising excessively heavy cargo. But it had to be readjusted before it could be used, and that would take at least one hour. Meanwhile, the humming of motors came into Hsiao's ears from the first and third hatches, but here in her second hatch the machines had been switched off. "Comrades, couldn't we speed up a bit?" Hsiao could not help asking, although she knew it was not so easy to solve the problem.

"We'll try our best to fix it in an hour," said a sailor.

An hour's halt in loading? No! Her thoughts began racing like the waves on the river. Everybody offered suggestions, but none of them was practical. And time was slipping by. Hsiao remained silent but her mind was active. She remembered that when she was moving something too heavy, other dockers would give her a hand. If a heavy object could be moved by two persons, why couldn't a piece of heavy cargo be lifted by two cranes?

She jumped to her feet and gave Chih-ying a punch. "I've got it! I've got it!" she exclaimed. Chih-ying stared at her, puzzled. Hsiao explained. Chih-ying nodded as she got the idea, then she took Hsiao by the hand. They went to see the Party secretary Wu and Old Kao, the dispatcher. They both shouted, "We've got an idea!" as they entered.

"Let me hear it," Wu said calmly.

"We can work two cranes simultaneously, can't we?"

"Of course. That's what several veteran dockers have just suggested."

"This is what they call: great minds think alike," Kao said.

Everyone discussed the possible difficulties and ways and means of overcoming them. In the end, Party Secretary Wu summed up, "Hsiao and Chih-ying, you must work in perfect co-ordination. We trust you will fulfil the task."

Chih-ying and Hsiao returned confidently to their posts.

Old Kao waved his hand to start. Two huge hooks descended slowly over the seven-ton piece, then remained suspended just above it. The dockers watched and commented, eyes full of trust and encouragement. The two hooks were put into the two loops of the lead cable on the piece. Hsiao's and Chih-ying's eyes met. Both nodded. They looked at Old Kao. The veteran worker gave the signal. The motors hummed, the lead cable tautened and the huge piece began to rise. The Party secretary Wu, standing by the cargo hatch, shot a glance of encouragement to the crane operators now and then. People's heart-strings tightened.

But no one was so stirred as the political commissar. The idea of using two cranes to lift such a big piece had not occurred to him. But the method worked. He glanced at Hsiao. The girl was all attention to Old Kao's signals, her lips pressed together. She seemed no different than before. What made her so clever today? Must have been Chairman Mao's works and Yeh's instruction. . . .

Just then Yeh arrived. He clasped the political commissar's hand, their eyes communicating with one another. Then they turned simultaneously to watch Hsiao. "Let's go to the operators' cab," said Yeh.

The huge crate suddenly gave a jerk. Old Kao promptly signalled the operators to stop and the girls promptly obeyed. The crate remained suspended in mid-air.

The political commissar also experienced a sense of suspension in his heart. Could Hsiao stand the trial? He flung a questioning look at Yeh. The veteran worker nodded.

Chih-ying's voice suddenly rang in the air, "my machine circuit has gone dead!" This was an accident, but not unexpected. In a few moments the circuit was on again. The crate began to descend through the hatch and safely landed in the hold. Then two free hooks emerged above the deck and slowly rose into the air. A tempest of cheering broke out in the crowd.

Hsiao smoothed her short hair back with a hand and heaved a sigh of relief. Only then did she notice that Yeh had come with a cup of tea for her while her father stood by, smiling. A host of mixed feelings overwhelmed her. Her lips trembled, but no words came. She took the tea and sipped. A wave of warmth diffused throughout her body.

S.S. Chang Feng heaved anchor, sounded its whistle and set sail early one morning in the glory of the fresh sun. As the ship moved slowly away from the pier, Party secretary Wu, Hsiao and Chih-ying stood waving a farewell to the leaving ship. Sea-gulls wheeled over the river searching for food. Suddenly they burst out in loud cries as if heralding the spring. Then they lifted themselves high in the air, flew over the *Chang Feng*, and out to sea. The ship stood out against a background of golden waves.

Party secretary Wu touched Hsiao's and Chih-ying's shoulders and, pointing to the gulls, said, "See what strong wings they have! They look far and fly far." The girls understood. They stood shoulder to shoulder, gazing into the distance, ready to receive assignments for new battles.

Illustrated by Chen Yu-hsien

The Call

Chu Yu-tung

As luck would have it, Wei Hua met Mama Chin as soon as he arrived by bus in New Village.

Wei and Mama Chin's son Yu-huan used to serve in the same company in the People's Liberation Army. Just a year before, Yu-huan had been transferred to work at battalion headquarters but the two of them, though separated, still belonged to the same battalion. Wei had heard that Yu-huan came home on furlough ten days previously. He therefore asked, "Where's Yu-huan, aunty?"

"There. . ." the old woman answered, pointing to the swirling dust on the road. "In today's last bus to town."

"On business?"

"Back to the battalion."

"Back to the battalion?" Wei was puzzled, for he knew that Yu-huan's holidays were not yet up.

Mama Chin produced a telegram from her pocket and handed it to Wei. "Have a look at this," she said, "it came at noon."

Wei unfolded it and read: "Emergency mission for whole battalion. Return at once." This was a surprise. Saying goodbye to Mama Chin, he hurried towards the post office at the west end of the village.

A girl was on duty behind the counter. "Comrade, is there a telegram for me?" Wei blurted as he strode in. The girl must have sensed the urgency in his voice as she looked up to scrutinize the PLA man standing before her. He had a travel-stained face, carrying a bag in one hand and a satchel slung across his shoulder. Apparently, he was on his way home.

"Comrade, will you first tell me your name and . . .?" the girl asked politely.

Wei flushed at his own rashness and quickly added, "I'm sorry. My name is Wei Hua. I'm from Weiwan Village."

The girl smiled and went into the inner room to check her records. Before long she came out, saying, "No, there's no telegram for you, comrade."

"Please notify me immediately if there is one."

Actually, this request was quite unnecessary for this post office was an advanced unit known throughout the province for the good work of its postmen. Newspapers, letters and parcels were handled with great accuracy. As for telegrams, they were always delivered promptly.

Wei left the post office but still felt a bit uneasy. "Since there is an emergency mission for the battalion, why's there no telegram for me?" he wondered as he walked off towards his village. "Perhaps it's because Yu-huan's at headquarters and I'm in the company. My telegram will likely arrive a bit later than his. It'll come this evening or tomorrow morning." As Wei Hua stepped out along the road Chairman Mao's words rang in his ears, **"Heighten our vigilance, defend the motherland."** He felt that this was a call to him, telling him he should not wait for the telegram asking him to return to his company. He put down his bag, fished out a Train and Boat Timetable from his pocket and studied it.

Unfortunately, all buses and boats had already left on their last trips. If it were earlier he could have gone back at once, but now he had to wait. The quickest way to get back was to take the 9:12 train the following morning at Hankow. So he decided to take his things home and have a meal first, then march twenty kilometres by night to the county town. From there he could catch the morning's first steamer, which would take him to Hankow by daybreak. . . . It was a well-thought-out plan. He hurried on his way.

*

In August, it is sultry in the south. Although it was near sunset and a soft breeze cooled his face,

Wei was hot and all of a sweat when he arrived at Weiwan, his home village.

Weiwan Village, beside a lake, was a fishing hamlet surrounded by water on three sides. "The Wei Peninsula," as people used to call it, was very beautiful. Before liberation, most of the villagers were fishermen and an old folk song of the poor fisherfolk is still deep in the villagers' memory:

> The boat floats with broken oars,
> We fishermen live on water;
> By day we are drenched in rain,
> At night in a rickety boat we huddle together.

After liberation the village changed greatly and the people began to farm so that they led a new and secure life. Now the fields were covered with golden ripening rice, the ears waving in the evening breeze, while the fragrance of water chestnuts and lotus drifted across the lake. It was a lovely waterside village!

However, Wei was in no mood to enjoy such beauty. He brooded as he eyed the misty lake, "If I can go by boat from here, it'll take me direct to Hankow. . . ." But he quickly abandoned the idea.

True enough, in the past, people visiting their families in Hankow, or going there to sell fish or buy goods, usually went by boat, for it only took five or six hours to row across the lake. Later, when a highway was built around the lake, they went to the city by bus via New Village. Though they had to walk some distance to reach the bus stop, it was still quicker and a more comfortable way to travel. They could make the trip and be back on the same day. Therefore, nowadays, except for those who took loads of lotus roots by boat to town or brought back fertilizer to the village, no one ever went by water any more even during the day. Naturally there was no boat going at night.

When Wei reached home, he found the door locked. His mother had not returned from the fields. He put down his bag beside the door, took out a few parcels and a notebook and went off to see the old Party secretary.

After her day's work Mother Wei started for home. A group of youngsters who had seen Wei ran to tell her, "Big Brother Hua's come home."

"Not really!" Mother thought to herself. "Didn't he say in his letter a few days ago that he wouldn't be coming back?" She hurried home and found her son's bag lying outside the door, but no son. From experience she knew where he must have gone. Previously, when Wei had come home on leave he would put down his bags and go off immediately. "When a soldier comes home, he should report to the local Party organization," he had said. "I must go to see the Party secretary first." No doubt, he must have gone to visit the old Party secretary now.

She unlocked the door, took his bag into the house and hurried to the kitchen. As she bustled about preparing a meal, she heard her son calling, "Ma!" She turned and there he was: her tall, good-looking son standing there in front of her. She was too happy for words. After a moment's silence, she asked, "Didn't you say you were too busy to come back?"

"My commanders and comrades are concerned about you and urged me to come back to see you," Wei explained. "They booked my ticket and arranged everything for me."

"How kind of them!" Mother's face was beaming as she resumed her cooking. From time to time she peeped at her strong, well-built PLA son, then suggested that he should change his sweat-sodden clothes. But he replied, "It doesn't matter. We soldiers are used to it." When Mother wanted to warm some water for her son to take a bath, he said, "No, mother, I've something more important to do after dinner." Mother thought her son had just become rather careless of his own appearance, she had no idea of the plan he had made.

By the time Mother put the washed rice into a pot to boil, it was already twilight and the chickens were returning to their coop. She went out into the yard and closed the coop. Wei followed her out.

"Do the wild cats still come to our coop, ma?" he asked, for he knew that these wild creatures used to steal some of their chickens.

"Yes," Mother answered. "Wild cats and skunks do sometimes find their way into the yard at night. We always have to be on the alert."

"Those rotten thieves! They steal in at night. : . ." Wei murmured thoughtfully, more or less to himself, rather than to his mother.

Mother did not notice her son's expression, she was absorbed in removing the top cover off the coop and stretching a hand in to catch a plump scarlet-combed cock. She wanted to kill it to make a special dish for her son. But before she could catch the rooster, Wei stopped her.

"Don't kill it, ma," he said. "An ordinary meal will do. I have to go right after dinner." He did not know that in his haste, he had made a slip of the tongue.

"What!" Mother was taken aback. "Where are you going when it's already so late?"

Wei tapped his forehead with his fingers as though regretting that he had let out his secret. Mother and son went back to the kitchen and, while helping her, he told her about his plan. He began with Yu-huan's telegram and how he had returned to his battalion promptly. Mother nodded approvingly as she listened. She praised Yu-huan and his mother for doing the right thing.

"You know, ma," Wei reminded her, "we led a dog's life before liberation. It's all due to the Party and Chairman Mao that I grew up and became a PLA fighter. I joined the Party and now I'm a political instructor. If the army has an emergency mission, it means the Party's calling us. D'you think I could remain at home? If the imperialists, revisionists and reactionaries are launching an attack on us, can we let these wild cats and skunks off with impunity?"

Busy cooking, Mother remained silent, mulling over every word her son said. She had made several dishes, including some egg soup. Thoughtfully she tasted each of them to see if they were what her son liked. She felt that her son was right and was particularly glad that he had not forgotten their class origin and their hatred of the oppressors for she still shuddered whenever she thought of the bitter past.

One autumn day the same year that Wei was born, a local gangster and his lackeys swarmed on board their dilapidated boat demanding a tax. Too poor to pay any, Wei's father argued with these heartless bullies. Because he did this, they knocked the poor fisherman off his boat into the lake and pounded him on the head with oars. Wei's poor father drowned. To keep her hatred alive, Mother gave Wei the name of "Oar". The following year, the people's army swept across the land, the People's Republic of China was established and the fishermen were freed from their oppressors. Mother knew it was the Party and Chairman Mao who had saved her son and hoping he would be able to serve his country well when he grew up, she changed his name from "Oar" to "Hua" — meaning China.

With this sad recollection Mother's eyes were moist. To hide her sadness from her son, she turned her back and pretended to wash some bowls.

"We've overthrown the landlords and local gangsters, ma," Wei said to comfort her. "But that's not enough. Only by wiping out all exploiters and oppressors from the globe can we poor working people enjoy a secure and happy life." Mother again nodded without a word.

At that moment the old Party secretary entered the house and from the outer room overheard some of the conversation between mother and son in the kitchen. Wei had told the old man that he was going back that same night. Afraid that the boy's mother would feel bad about this, the old Party secretary had hurried over his own meal and come to help persuade the old woman. Since mother and son were still talking, he did not want to interrupt them, so he sat down in the outer room, filled his pipe and began to smoke. On the wall opposite him there was a picture taken from the revolutionary Peking opera *Taking Tiger Mountain by Strategy*. He stared at it and saw written beneath it: "A Communist always heeds the Party's call." He thought, "Wei is right to go back immediately."

In the kitchen, mother and son were still talking.

"Listen son, I don't mean that I won't let you go." That was Mother. "But you haven't received either a telegram or a letter asking you to go back. You've only got wind of it, so why are you in such a hurry?"

Wei was prepared for this. "Ma," he explained patiently, "I've already told you Yu-huan's telegram said: emergency mission for whole battalion. I'm in one of the battalion's companies. That means our company has an emergency mission too. You know, ma, when we soldiers are given a new task, we don't sit still."

"I know," Mother smiled. "I won't keep you long. But you must be tired now after that long journey in the bus and then walking here on foot. Have a night's rest at home and start back early tomorrow morning. That'll be more convenient than walking at night."

"I'd better go tonight, ma. We PLA men take action as soon as an order's given. That's our tradition." As he added another handful of fuel to the fire, the steam curled up from under the lid of the rice pot and an appetizing aroma filled the room.

What could a mother say to such a son? She could only agree with him. "All right, all right," she said. "Have your dinner and you can go!" She took the lid off the rice pot. "*Aiya!*" she cried. "With all this talk I nearly let the rice burn!" She began to laugh.

The old Party secretary walked into the kitchen. "It was a fine talk, sister," he said to Mother. "Hua is certainly a qualified political instructor. Every word he said hit the nail on the head. It didn't take him long to make his mother listen to reason." He laughed together with her.

"Hua's uncle, do you think I need him to give me a political talk?" Mother joked as she offered the old man a chair. "I understand Hua and why he insists on going back. He was only seventeen when he joined the PLA. Because he is my only son, my opinion was asked for. Did I say a word against his joining up? Don't you remember, old secretary?"

Of course he did. He not only remembered that moving scene, but also what happened later on. Last spring, though Wei had leave for fifteen days, he spent his time at home helping to train the village militia. Mother said not a word against it, but supported him throughout.

"Are you praising your son or yourself, sister?" the old Party secretary asked.

"Neither," Mother chuckled. "Too much praise makes one conceited. If he listens to Chairman Mao and works well, I'm satisfied." Then she turned to Wei and urged, "What are you waiting for, son? Start eating, then you can be on your way. Come on and join him, old secretary." Saying this, Mother went out. Neither of the men guessed what she was up to.

*

After the meal, the old Party secretary and the young political instructor talked about the village militia. Before long Mother returned with two oars. "Get your things ready, Hua," she ordered. "I'll have a quick bite and then row you across the lake. It's better than your walking in the dark to town and still possibly missing the first steamer there." She stood the oars up against the wall as she spoke.

Both the old Party secretary and Wei were astonished. They had never thought of her doing such a thing. Actually, when the old Party secretary went over he not only thought he would help Wei persuade his mother but also intended to accompany the young PLA man on his nocturnal march to town. Now Mother, by her quick action, had gone a step ahead of him.

Wei understood his mother as well as she understood him. Once a decision was made, she never changed it. He looked long at his mother's receding back not knowing what to say, then he began to put his things together. There really was not much for him to do. Just leave his mother the things he had bought for her and ask the old Party secretary to pass on the gifts to some old people in the village. As for the books the militiamen had asked him to buy, he had already left them with the Party secretary. His clean underwear was still in his satchel.

Having finished her meal, Mother came out of the kitchen to the outer room. She took the hurricane-lamp down from its post, filled it with kerosene, trimmed the wick and lit it. She flipped some dust off her tunic, rolled up her sleeves and said, "Let's go!" Briskly, she stepped out of the house.

Mother led the way till the three of them came to the lake, then mother and son jumped into a small boat, unmoored it and made off. Standing quietly on the bank, the Party secretary gazed at it disappearing in the darkness and listened to the sound of the oars in the water. Suddenly a bicycle bell tinkled behind him and a girl shouted, "Comrade — Wei —

Hua —" The voice sounded familiar, but the old secretary did not recognize it for a moment.

The girl rode up and jumped off her bicycle, calling loudly, "Old secretary!"

"Is that you Young Lo?" the old man asked.

Young Lo was the girl Wei had spoken to in the post office when he arrived at New Village. "Just now we received a telegram for Comrade Wei Hua," she gasped, still out of breath. "I hurried to his house but nobody was in. A neighbour told me he'd just left for the lake, so I came on here." She handed the telegram to the old secretary.

The old man took it. In the light of the girl's flashlight, he tore it open and read: "Emergency mission for whole battalion. Return at once." Pointing to the telegram, he said smiling, "Young Lo, yours is an advanced post office. But this time you've lagged behind."

"What? He's gone!"

"Yes." The old secretary pointed to the lake, over which hung a curtain of evening mist, but the dipping of the oars in the water could still be heard faintly in the distance, where the glimmer of the small hurricane-lamp still showed. A full moon was rising, its silvery rays etching the willows and reeds along the bank. Even the distant hills seemed near. The night was calm and beautiful.

The girl understood completely and with some emotion she said, "PLA men always answer the Party's call promptly."

Illustrated by Chen Yu-hsien

Spring Comes to a Fishing Village

Hung Shan

This spring I was on my way to the Changpai Mountains just when they were turning a fresh pale green. The spring fishing season had just begun. The weather was fine just as it had been when I went there twenty-six years ago.

I was going to the small fishing village of Chiangnantun, on the south side of the Tanchiang River which people referred to as "the hamlet across the river."

The heroic people of Chiangnantun had left an indelible impression on me though I spent no more than a few hours there years before when the flames of the anti-Japanese war raged across the land. I wondered whether the old Party secretary was still alive. And what had happened to the girl who I knew only by her pet name of Erh-wa?

The moon was already sailing over the mountain tops and the fishing boats were safely moored when I hurried to the ferry. Passers-by had told me that I need only shout "Sister-in-law Ma" and she would come to ferry me across.

The moonlight silhouetted the neat village homesteads situated on the southern river bank; their myriad lamps glittering like stars — a really pleasant sight!

Cupping my hands around my mouth I called, "Sister-in-law Ma" and heard my voice echoing through the mountains.

There was no reply. What bad luck! Suppose I couldn't get across? Where could I pass the night? Again I cupped my hands and yelled, "Sister. . . ." A ripple of clear laughter came from the willows on the opposite bank.

"Don't worry. I'm coming," someone answered crisply.

I heard the thud of ropes being thrown into a boat and saw a woman leap nimbly in too. She was obviously an old hand at the job. Look at the way she thrust the bamboo pole into the water, bending low as she strained against the current. The boat flew straight as an arrow towards me. Half way across she began to sing:

> Spring has come to the river banks,
> The bright sun shines warm in my heart.
> Continuing the revolution I drive ahead,
> The Tachai spirit prevails generation after generation.

I could feel her enthusiasm and optimism in the way she sang.

As the boat neared the bank, she used the pole skilfully so that the boat swerved to the right. Then with one more thrust of the pole from the prow she steadied it for me by the bank.

"Come along, please!" she said politely as she gave me a quick glance.

Heading towards the opposite bank, the boat skimmed the dark rippling water like a swallow as she poled vigorously, gripping the long pole in her big strong hands.

I sat opposite watching her in the increasing brightness of the moonlight. She was a sturdy, middle-aged woman, her hair bobbed and her skin dark from exposure to all sorts of weather. She seemed extremely strong. She must have been working in the fields for her clothes and shoes were muddy. Then, I noticed she was eyeing me too.

"Are you here for the first time?" she inquired.

"No, the second."

"Really? But it's impossible!" She looked me over again and laughed, shaking her head. "I remember all the people who've been here."

"But it was more than twenty years ago. . . ."

"Ah, that explains it." She smoothed her wind-ruffled hair. "Are you visiting some relatives, or are you here on business?"

"Neither. I've just come to see some old comrades."

"Who? I know everyone in the village, grown-ups and kids."

I could not tell her. I had not asked the names of the old secretary and the young girl I'd met in the few hours I was there the last time. "I want to see the old Party secretary and . . . ," I faltered.

"The old Party secretary?" She laughed again. "We've had several old secretaries since liberation. What was the name of your old secretary?"

I didn't know. I was trying to explain when suddenly one or two fish leaped out of the water. Quick as lightning she flung down the pole and grabbed a three-pronged fishing fork, waiting for the next fish to leap. Swish! The fork flew from her hand.

"It's a carp, about four pounds," she said, as she hauled it in. The fish thrashed about, till she threw it with a thud, together with the fork, into the boat. Once more she took up the pole.

I was amazed at her skill. Could she be. . . ?

"Comrade, I'd like to ask you about someone," I began. "One night twenty-six years ago, at this same ferry, a teen-aged girl ferried me across and she sang: 'More severe than winter is this spring, when will a real spring come to our Chiangnantun?'"

I noticed that she looked pensive.

"The girl was called Erh-wa," I continued.

"Ah!" She stared at me in surprise for a long while, but when she finally recognized me she threw down her pole and grasped my hand. "Are you Padlock?"

*

One spring night twenty-six years before, I had to pass through this small fishing hamlet on an important mission. I was told to look out for Erh-wa who would ferry me across the river.

The night was filled with the sound of the shrill wind and the waves crashing wildly against the river bank, as I waited for the girl. Then what I saw horrified me. On the opposite shore fire began to spread in the fishing village lighting up half the sky. There was the rattle of rifle shots. Dogs barked, while Japanese soldiers yelled. The thought of the horrors they had brought to the Chinese people filled me with rage as I hid in the grass by the bank. I heard another volley of shots, this time in the far distance, and realized that our own guerrillas were coming.

Suddenly, two Japanese soldiers came to the river bank, pushing a girl they brought with them and gesturing to her to ferry them across.

The girl, her head raised in a determined way, jumped into a boat. The waves were high. As the boat reached the middle of the river, she poled swiftly to the right while stepping suddenly to the other side of the boat so that it capsized in the fast-flowing water. With a big plop, the two soldiers fell overboard. But the girl, apparently a skilful swimmer, quickly righted the boat and, the next moment, she stood up proudly again.

The two Japanese soldiers swam well too. Soon, a black muzzle emerged to the water surface pointing at her. Quicker than it takes to tell, a glittering three-pronged fishing fork flew from her hands and landed square in the middle of his forehead. His lifeless body was tossed about by the tumbling waves until it disappeared in the swift current. The other soldier, who had surfaced behind the girl, also took aim. At this critical moment someone else emerged behind him and with a strong big hand forced his head back underneath the water. There was a brief struggle below the surface but only for a moment. Both the enemy soldiers were drowned.

The girl looked around, saw and understood everything; the old secretary had swum after the boat to protect her.

"Old Party secretary," the girl sobbed.

"That was a narrow escape, wasn't it, Erh-wa!" the old secretary admitted as he clambered onto the boat and looked at her lovingly.

The look reminded her of the important mission. She looked around quickly and sang:

> More severe than winter is this spring,
> When will a real spring come to our Chiangnantun?

This was my signal. That same night the two of them escorted me to my destination.

We chatted quietly on the way. When I looked at Erh-wa I thought her expression far too severe for a girl her age. "How's your mother?" I asked. There was no answer, she bit her lips and stared into vacant space.

The old secretary sighed and answered for her. "When there was a famine her family left their home village to try to make a living here in the Northeast. But her mother died of hunger on the way."

"What about your father?"

I heard a sob and regretted my thoughtless question.

"He died two years ago," the old secretary spoke indignantly. "Her father worked all his life for the tyrant who ruled our fishing village yet he never had a good feed of fish. When he was dying he craved for some fresh fish. Erh-wa forked one by moonlight and boiled it. But when she took it to her father, she found he was already dead."

My eyes smarted.

"That evil old blood-sucker arrived immediately and claimed that the death of Erh-wa's father was caused by the vengeance of the fish-god because the girl caught a fish without asking the god's permission. Besides, it was against the old despot's regulations too, so he said she must be punished. 'All right, go on and punish me,' Erh-wa retorted, the bowl of steaming fish soup still in her hands. The next moment she threw the whole bowl of it into the face of this old living monster. Fortunately that night our guerrillas killed him and avenged us all."

I finished my errand that same night before dawn. When I was leaving, Erh-wa said to me, "Take me to the people's army with you, please."

"But they need reliable people here too, and the old secretary needs a helper. Besides, you are the leader of the children's corps. How can you leave them?"

For a while she played with the end of her plait silently. "When will the Japanese be driven away?" she asked.

"Not long now!" I took out a copy of Chairman Mao's *On Protracted War* and gave it to her. "This was written by Chairman Mao. Read it and you will learn many things."

"Is it written by Chairman Mao?" Tears sparkled in her eyes as she clutched the book tightly to her.

*

What a coincidence that we should meet again now at the same ferry after so many years. We entered the village chatting gaily.

"The old secretary is still very spry. When his wife died three years ago I invited him to come and stay with us. I've looked after him like a father ever since."

Her face lit up when I asked about her family. "My husband is away at a meeting in the county town. My son is in the People's Liberation Army and my daughter's in middle school. After liberation I chose a name for myself. Now I'm called Chiang Fan."

"That's a beautiful name."

"Here we are!" She shouted into the house, "Father, who do you think's come to see us?"

The old grey-haired secretary, whose hearing and eyesight were still good, was delighted to talk. "I never dreamed of seeing you again, Padlock," he cried out, using my childhood name, after we refreshed his memory of our first encounter by mentioning the two Japanese soldiers.

"Father! We're all grown-ups now," Chiang Fan reminded him.

"Yes, it must be my age," the old man said apologetically.

"Oh, that's all right. It makes me feel like one of the family," I joked. "But my real name is Liu Li-hsin."

Just then a girl came in and called, "Secretary Chiang, we're all waiting for you."

"All right. I'll be along right away." Before Chiang Fan left she told her daughter to cook the fish so that the old secretary and I could have a meal together with some wine.

"Don't worry, mother, I've just put it on the stove. It'll be ready quite soon."

"So Chiang Fan is the Party secretary now," I said.

"Ah, yes." The old man was very proud of his adopted daughter. "She is a good leader of the poor and lower-middle peasants, busy all day long, rain or shine. Our village has changed a great deal since she was elected Party secretary." He became enthusiastic at the very mention of Chiang Fan's name.

"Grandfather, hasn't mother asked you not to praise her any more?" the girl reminded him.

"But if I don't tell Uncle Liu these things, how will he ever know?" the old man retorted.

"Before liberation, when this fishing village was ruled by an old tyrant, we had nothing to eat but ground acorns and corncobs. At that time people said, 'The fishermen are ground down just like the acorns and corncobs they have to eat.' Our life has changed so much since liberation. We're now masters of our country and we have enough food and clothing and lead an entirely different life.

"Chiang Fan was elected secretary of the Party branch during the Cultural Revolution. One day, pointing to the uncultivated land around our village she said to the poor and lower-middle peasants, 'This land, won with the blood of revolutionary martyrs, is now ours. But it still remains untouched, fertile as it is. Is it because we fishermen are too lazy? No. It is because we were prevented from working it by Liu Shao-chi's agents in agricultural departments who claimed that we should stick to fishing only and then we'd have everything we needed. This was wicked nonsense. Apart from fulfilling our fishing quota why shouldn't we go in for farming while it is possible? Chairman Mao says: **Take grain as the key link and ensure an all-round development.** We must have a broader perspective.'

"In early spring, Chiang Fan took the lead and, with a pick, began to break up the frozen soil. She never rested a single day though her hands blistered till they bled and her arms were swollen. When the snow melted, standing in the icy water for several hours at a stretch, she led the commune members to build water conservancy projects. She often said: We mustn't take grain from the state any more when we have such a rich granary right here."

Pointing with his chopsticks at the rice in his bowl, the old man went on, "Ours was a fishing village in the past. Now we're farming as well. We grew this rice. Isn't it fine?"

He became more and more enthusiastic as he talked. Waving his hand, he went on, "In the past few years, besides fulfilling our fishing quota and having plenty of grain for ourselves, we've delivered more than 100,000 pounds of grain to the state."

"That's wonderful!"

"Well, no! Chiang Fan says that our contribution to the state is still too little. We must exert ourselves and look out for conceit and self-complacency."

*

Overcome by fatigue I fell asleep for a while but woke up again at ten o'clock. Chiang Fan was reading at her desk.

"You're not in bed yet, Comrade Chiang," I said drowsily.

"No, did I disturb you?"

"She always studies before she goes to bed every night," the old man explained.

"Oh, skip it, father," Chiang Fan said.

"But it's the truth." The old man smiled. "Look, she's been working at the dam all day, attended a meeting this evening, and still. . . ."

"Sister-in-law Ma." A clear voice rang out from the other bank.

Chiang Fan put down her book immediately and went out.

"Is there no ferryman?" I asked the old man.

"Yes. But he lives farther away while we're so close to the river. Besides, if anyone needs the ferry at night it must be on urgent work. How can a leader stay at home and not go out to take care of such people?"

Now I can see the whole picture. As I watched Chiang Fan hurrying to the ferry in the moonlight, I recalled the song she sang earlier in the evening:

> Spring has come to the river banks,
> The bright sun shines warm in my heart.
> Continuing the revolution I drive ahead,
> The Tachai spirit prevails generation after generation.

Now in this great Mao Tsetung era spring belongs to us. It will always be ours.

Illustrated by Huang Chia-yu

The Ferry at Billows Harbour

Fang Nan

On a bright spring day in March I arrived once again on the shores of the East China Sea. My destination was Langkangyu, a place to which I had longed for years to return.

Unfortunately, on the morning I was due to start out there was a windstorm. According to the comrades at the local weather station, it would gain in momentum that day. This worried me. If the gale continued for several days, I should be held up there. With a mind to try my luck, I started out early in the morning for the ferry at Billows Harbour.

Not a soul was in sight on the wharf, by the rocks or along the beach. Across the turbulent sea there was not a single boat to be seen. Only a few sea-gulls braved the wind as they soared and hung in the cloud-laden sky. Huge combers, lace-edged with froth and spume, raced up the beach, sweeping up and spewing out sand and pebbles as they crashed thunderously on the shore.

Impatiently I stood watching the surf break on the stony beach. Suddenly, a giant breaker crashed its head on a nearby rock, showering salt sea-water all over me. Far in the distance, I could vaguely see the outline of Langkangyu Island and haunting memories swirled into my mind as turbulently as the sea churned before my eyes. There, from Langkangyu, I had started out once on an unforgettable journey across the sea. . . .

It was early in 1950, on the eve of the Choushan Islands' liberation, when the fisherfolk were still suffering untold miseries. After an ignominious defeat on the mainland, Chiang Kai-shek's bandit troops beat a hasty retreat and entrenched themselves on the hundreds of small isles which constitute the fishing grounds known as Choushan. The Eastern Chekiang Special Committee of the Communist Party sent dozens of liaison men out to the islands to investigate conditions there so that the local Party organizations could support the Chinese People's Liberation Army when its expeditionary forces crossed the sea to wipe out these bandit remnants. I was one of these scouts. Langkangyu, where I was sent, was a strategic island and therefore one of our main battle targets. Soon after my arrival I made contact with our underground communications man old Ming-hai, and with his able assistance I obtained most of the needed information.

Shortly before I was due to leave the island, there was an unexpected turn of events. Bandit troops blockaded the ferry and grounded all boats. In collusion with the local despots, they searched the island with a fine tooth-comb. I was already near the beach at the time and when I saw what was happening, I turned round and raced for the rock-bound far end of the island. From a distance enemy soldiers fired a few volleys at me and, unfortunately, just as I was clambering over a high rock, a bullet nicked me in the left shoulder. At this critical moment a big hand from above hauled me up. Its owner rolled me onto his back and quickly carried me into a hidden cave farther in among the rocks. When he finally put me down, I recognized the face of old Ming-hai. He bound up my wound but had to leave me again for, since the situation had taken this sudden turn, in spite of the risk to his own safety, he needed to gain more information for me. Before the old man disappeared we agreed to meet again that evening in the same cave.

Cooped up there, I was torn by anxiety. According to plan I was to take what information I had gathered to the Party Committee that very evening. The wind increased at dusk and soon became a real gale. Giant waves pounded nearer and nearer until some crashed right into the cave. Worry overwhelmed me as I watched the maelstrom. Suddenly, I heard a seagull's cry. That was our signal. I answered promptly. As a shadow flitted near and entered the mouth of the cave, I rushed towards it. To my astonishment, it was not old Ming-hai but a young fisherwoman, a baby strapped to her back. She wore a brown jacket and the customary wide trousers. Her jet black hair was knotted at the nape of her neck in the local style and a little red flower was tucked in it. A pair of ear-rings made of bright silk thread hung from her ears and a small blue apron was tied around her waist. She was barefooted. "I'm Ah-chu, comrade. Uncle Ming-hai sent me," she said to introduce herself as she deftly pulled out a small wad of paper from her knot of hair and handed it to me. It contained all the information I needed.

"Where's Uncle Ming-hai?" I asked anxiously.

Ah-chu was silent for a second, quite obviously having to compose herself. She told me then how old Ming-hai had been captured on his way back to me after having obtained the needed information. Though he was cruelly tortured, he refused to reveal any hint as to my whereabouts and they beat him until he lost consciousness. Yet in spite of all this, he had found a way to send the information I needed by this young woman. I was so enraged that I pulled out my pistol. "Where have they put old uncle?" I demanded, longing to wipe out those beasts there and then.

Ah-chu's intelligent glance halted me. "You've to cross the sea tonight, comrade," she sighed.

I gradually controlled my anger. "But we've no boat. Even if we can find one, how shall we cross this stormy sea?" My heart was very heavy.

"On the contrary," said Ah-chu brightly. "The storm will help us. Otherwise, I don't know how we'd ever find a boat." I was quite at a loss to know what she meant.

Without pausing to explain, she glanced at me again, then hurriedly unstrapping the baby from her back, she put it in my arms. "You wait," was all she said before she disappeared. "Where . . . are. . . ." But before I could question her there was a splash as she dived into the rolling waves. My heart sank again.

I hugged Ah-chu's small daughter tight. She looked very like her mother. A bright silver necklet flashed against her scarlet coat and from one chubby little wrist dangled two pretty sea shells which gleamed like gems. With bright eyes she stared at the sea into which her mother had disappeared.

Darkness came followed by the rising tide. The gale continued and the sea grew wilder. Not another sound came across the water from the isle occupied by the Kuomintang bandits.

After an hour or so, a small sampan suddenly appeared at the cave entrance. Ah-chu climbed in, took up the baby and, as she strapped the child onto her back, she ordered, "Quick, comrade, get on board." She was very firm.

"Did you get it from the ferry?" I asked, jumping on board.

"Yes. I swam close to the wharf and peered around. The bandits, sheltering their faces in their coat collars, were milling around the dock," Ah-chu replied as she jumped onto the boat. "Go ahead and mill around, you gangsters, I thought. I've work to do. And so I quietly untied a sampan, weighed anchor and towed the boat out."

Ah-chu's description sounded so simple, but well I knew the hazards of swimming out in this wild stormy sea and then towing a boat out from that wolves' lair so closely patrolled. It was an extremely dangerous exploit.

The sampan flew in the direction of the ferry. The howling wind and raging seas surrounded us like an ominous net but our little boat rushed bravely ahead. From time to time, I turned around to look at the young fisherwoman wrestling with the waves. Fear gripped me, mostly for the baby strapped to her back who seemed to feel the fury of wind and water.

Our sampan had barely got over a maelstrom when Ah-chu cried out: "A gunboat!"

I listened intently. True enough, above the howling wind I vaguely made out the roar of a motor. Immediately, a shaft of white light cut across the darkness, piercing the dark gloomy night, and swept towards us. I pulled out my pistol, ready to fight it

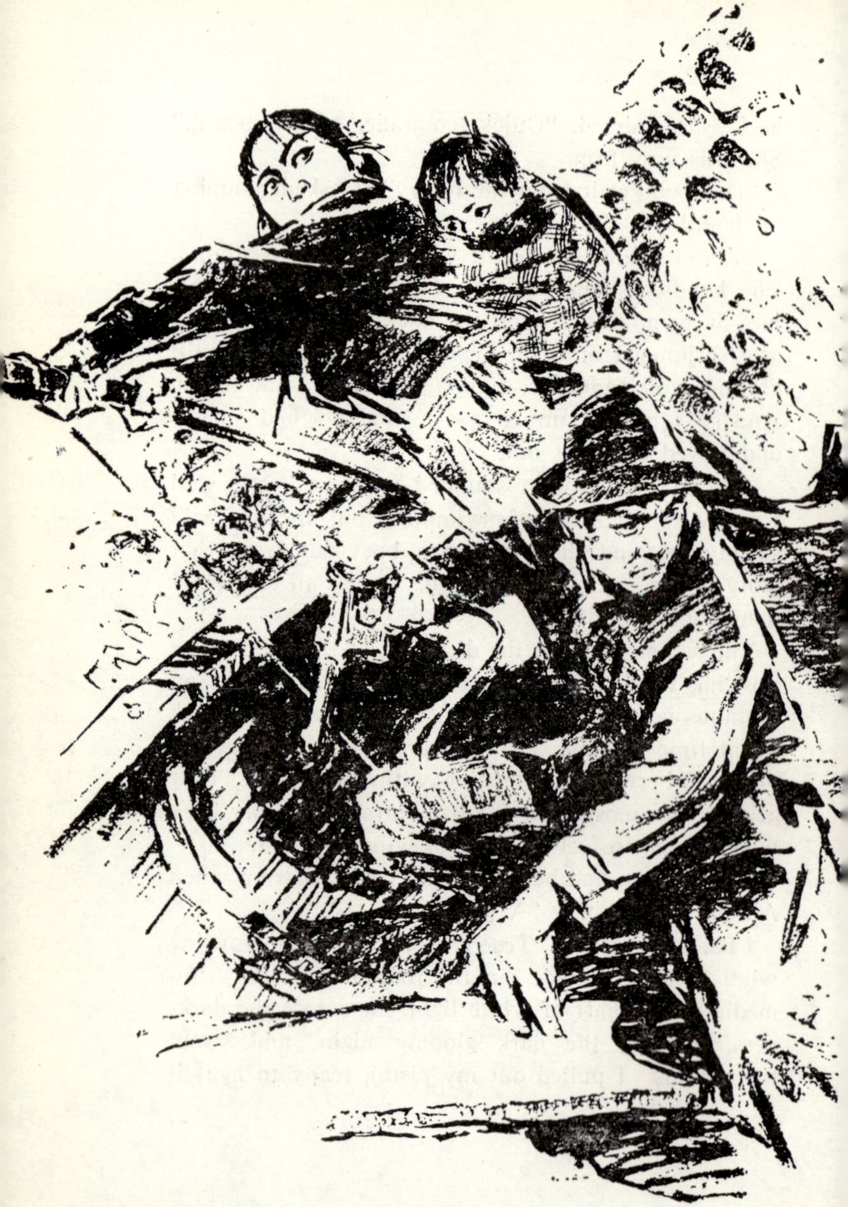

out with them. At this critical moment Ah-chu swung the rudder vigorously, bending in her efforts and, as the boat swerved sharply to the right, we glided quickly into a channel between the reefs. The light flickered on the rocks all around us.

I gaped at what the light revealed. What a weird place it was. Towering, sharp-edged rocks surrounded us as our sampan whirled through the narrow channel between them. Ah-chu, however, was quite unperturbed. Both hands on the rudder, she manoeuvred the boat as it flew along on the tide. After about half an hour's wrestling, we finally escaped from this weird rock-bound place.

"Where were we?" I asked, turning for a final look at those piles of odd-looking rock formations.

"They're the Tiger-Head Reefs!"

"Tiger-Head Reefs," I repeated in awe.

After three hours or so of battling wind and sea, Ah-chu brought me to the mainland. Wiping the mingled sweat and sea-water from her dripping face, she said, "We're sinking in a sea of misery, comrade. We look forward every minute and every hour for our own army to come and liberate us."

"It won't be long now, Comrade Ah-chu," I assured her, as I pressed her burning hands. I wanted her and the baby to stay and return to the island until the storm subsided. Ah-chu only smiled and said, "Don't worry about us, comrade. We grew up on the salt waves of these island seas." Before saying goodbye I looked at the baby with a special fondness.

She was sleeping soundly, still strapped to her mother's back. A few drops of sea-water sliding towards her baby lips parted in sleep sparkled on her fat cheeks....

*

That happened more than twenty years ago. Since then, I'd gone here and there as work demanded but never had the chance to return to Langkangyu, nor did I meet this brave fisherwoman again. Whenever I thought of the sea or if friends mentioned it, memory recalled this courageous woman and her baby daughter. They flashed into my mind's eye linked with the shores of the East China Sea.

My mind now turned to my immediate task, which was to cross to the island. It looked as if it would be impossible to go right then. Perhaps I had better wait in my hostel in the county town. Before I set off I took one last look at the tossing sea. Suddenly, for a brief second, I spotted a flash of red. In contrast to the wide expanse of foam-flecked waves the bright red showed up like a spray of red plum blossoms in a snowy scene. That red dot rose and fell with the heaving combers, now climbing a crest, now dropping out of sight in a trough. It came nearer and nearer until I saw clearly that it was a red jacket worn by a young girl.

She stood erect on a tiny sampan, a five-foot rifle slung across one shoulder. Braving the wind, the boat was sailing straight for Billows Harbour Ferry. I soon made out two other girls on the small craft:

one in a sky blue jacket, the other in a pale green one. All three girls were armed.

Overjoyed, I ran towards the wharf. But I had barely reached it when I noticed that about two hundred yards off the shore the sampan suddenly turned. I snatched off my cap and started to wave frantically. After a few seconds the boat swung around again and came towards the ferry landing. About twenty yards from the shore, the sails were lowered.

"Hey there, comrade, where d'you want to go?"

"Langkangyu Island. . . ." I shouted back.

"What for?"

"I've business with the revolutionary committee."

The girls looked me over vigilantly, then they took up oars and poles to bring the sampan to shore. Because the sea was so rough the girls had a hard time bringing the boat to the wharf. As I stood there fretting, the girl in the red jacket who was steering, turned the rudder sharply, following the upward swell of a wave and the boat slipped along beside a jutting rock close to the wharf. I jumped in quickly, but before I could get my balance, the sampan tipped sharply and I nearly fell overboard. A strong hand steadied me just in time. It was the girl in red. I nodded my thanks. She only smiled as she said, "Be careful, comrade, you must stand firmly on such a rolling sea." Then, continuing in the same polite manner, she asked: "Have you a letter of introduction, comrade?"

"Of course," I replied and quickly showed her my papers. She looked them over and handed them back still smiling.

Then all three girls set to work. One started poling, another used an oar. They bustled about on the small craft quite steadily as if they were on land. "Raise the sail," commanded the girl in red as she kept one hand on the rudder and with the other pulled at the sail rope. The other two raised the jib and, humming a work song together, they hoisted it up in less than a minute. All this they did in close co-ordination and perfect timing, each of them working so skilfully that I was really impressed.

The girl in red, likely in her early twenties, seemed to be the eldest. With lively eyes, thick eyebrows and a high bridge on an oblong face, she looked quite intelligent and strong-willed. With her right hand, she kept a firm grip on the rudder while still holding the sail rope, as she directed the sampan on its course. Though still so young, her every movement was that of a veteran seaman used to roughing it on the sea. I was told her name was Hai-ying (Sea Blossom). Her two companions were Shui-chu (Water Pearl) and Hai-hua (Flower of the Sea).

"Must be your first journey on such a rough sea, eh comrade?" asked Hai-ying, glancing at me. "How are you feeling?"

I had to admit honestly that I was a little tense. In my turn, I glanced at them one by one and couldn't help asking, "Where are you girls going, fully armed like this?"

"Target shooting," they answered in unison.

"But can you do that in this storm?" I asked, very surprised.

"Why not? We pick days like this to go out on the sea for target shooting," Hai-ying told me. "You see, there's nothing frightening about the sea. As for wind and waves, there's nothing to them either. Although they appear fierce, they're actually paper tigers. As long as you know all about them and dare to struggle against them, they're easy to tame."

The sampan sailed against the wind. Shui-chu and Hai-hua took up their rifles, then knelt down on one knee. Seeing that they were taking careful aim, I looked in the same direction. After careful searching, I saw a tiny target in the distance no bigger than a bean, which bobbed up and down, now distinct, now blurred.

I said apologetically to Hai-ying, "I'm afraid that ferrying me across is keeping you from your militia exercises."

Hai-ying shook her head. "Not a bit of it. Your coming is just right, for we intended to practise crossing too."

"Crossing?" I was surprised again. Hai-ying's reply was clear-cut. "Yes. Our instructor told us that since we are a sea-borne militia we must learn to shoot well in a storm and steer steadily in a gale."

"Oh, steer steadily in a gale," I repeated.

"That's it," said Hai-ying excitedly. "Our instructor was telling us only yesterday that we must practise steering through violent storms so that we won't lose our course under any conditions. We should be able not only to brave fierce gales and towering waves, but navigate through dangerous rocky channels and treacherous reefs too. Only then shall we become skilled navigators and be able to go wherever we please."

"Well said, Comrade Hai-ying," I cried. "Count on me then as a new militiaman in your exercise."

"Then you must give us plenty of advice," answered Hai-ying delightedly.

We were now half-way to the island. Suddenly, an unexpected blast pressed down on us and the sampan tipped to one side. Water streamed in. The wind was getting stronger and the waves were higher. Hai-ying looked up at the sky, then out to sea.

"Comrades," she began shouting orders for the exercise. "The enemy has blocked our course across the sea to Langkangyu. We must change our direction immediately. We shall turn northwest, stem the wind and tide and slip along the channel through Tiger-Head Reefs." So saying, with both hands on the rudder, she turned the sampan at a ninety degree angle. Shui-chu and Hai-hua stopped their target practice, jumped to their feet and made ready for action.

Tiger-Head Reefs! My pulse quickened at the name. What a coincidence that I was to go through those dangerous reefs a second time.

After our sampan changed its course we sailed towards Tiger-Head Reefs, bucking the storm. As most sailors know, the most difficult navigation is against a head wind. Right then, our craft was sailing against the tide also. It was difficult to make much headway. We zigzagged along for about thirty minutes when about two hundred yards ahead of us a stretch of white foam caught my eye. It looked as if there were thousands of sharks frisking just under the surface of the sea. The waves crashed with such a thunderous roar that even from this distance I realized we were nearing Tiger-Head Reefs. My! Those gigantic rock formations looked really hazardous, just like so many jagged tigers' teeth. Between the protruding rocks and hidden reefs lay a narrow navigable channel which wound its way around them. Wind-borne combers and the rushing tide joined to form a swirling current which surged through the narrow channel. It was evident that to sail through it we might run the risk of being tossed into the undertow and swallowed or crushed against the rocks. As we neared the reefs, I asked Hai-ying, "Have you sailed through here before?"

"Yes," said Hai-ying. "But never in weather like this."

I tried sounding her out further. "There's a strong gale and we're going against the tide too. Are you sure you can make it?"

"Sure!" Hai-ying gave me a swift glance out of the corner of her eyes. "You know you can't seize a tiger cub unless you dare to venture into the tiger's lair. Since we must tame Tiger-Head Reefs, we need the guts to navigate this channel. In case of war, the enemy won't pick good weather to invade. Isn't that so, comrade?"

"Good for you. So you're actually following the old saying, 'Going into tiger mountain, knowing full well there are tigers there.' Isn't that so?" Hai-ying smiled at me, a smile both confident and full of pride.

"Comrades, we're now approaching the channel," announced Hai-ying as our sampan skirted a half-hidden reef and entered a narrow waterway. Huge rocks with razor-sharp edges reared up on either side of our boat as it skimmed over a swirling undertow. Hai-ying steered competently, looking quite unruffled as the sampan twisted on its way, in spite of the swift current, now skirting a rock, now rounding a hidden reef. Riding the combers, we shot right into the howling wind. Soon, half the course was behind us and we reached a sharp turn.

"Enemy strafing has broken our main mast," Hai-ying announced suddenly. The other two girls leapt into action. With a swish, they lowered the main sail and mast. The sampan slowed down. The girls quickly seized the oars and began to row vigorously.

I too scampered up to the bow, grabbed an oar and pitched in. Hai-ying continued to steer, keeping us steadily on course. The little sampan resumed its journey.

After about an hour's hard work, we approached the last difficult channel in the Tiger-Head Reefs known as the Tiger's Jaws. It was also the most dangerous. Four giant rocks reared up out of the water like enormous fangs, each edged with foaming white spray. Concave below, they almost formed an arch above, very much like the jaws of a tiger, while countless waves poured in and out between them.

As a rapid current lessened, I spied in the distance a dark mass much like the remains of a big shark which was impaled there. The Tiger's Jaws were divided by it into two halves. When I pointed to it, Hai-ying shouted to tell me that it was the wreck of a Kuomintang gunboat. In the early days right after liberation when our brave People's Liberation Army men were still pursuing remnants of the Kuomintang bandit troops as they fled south in a desperate attempt to escape, an enemy gunboat tried to make a get-away by rushing through the Tiger-Head Reefs. Sailing at full speed into the Tiger's Jaws, it was rammed by a rock and smashed, some pieces sinking, but some still remaining above water. That, of course, was years and years ago and one rusty part of the boat still stuck up in the channel. Hai-ying's description of the bandits' desperate flight amused me. But what I feared was that this rusty piece of the wrecked ship had become another iron tooth set into the tiger's jaws, making it more difficult for our sampan to pass through. I glanced back at Hai-ying. She was standing firm looking as determined as ever. I knew that my apprehension on her behalf was quite unnecessary.

When our sampan was about thirty yards or so from the Tiger's Jaws, we all pitched in with the oars, in an attempt to rush through the channel, but the wind and tide swept us back again and again.

Hai-ying's brows were gathered in a frown, as she looked thoughtfully at the Tiger's Jaws. Then, pushing back a lock of wet hair from her forehead, she shouted at us: "Comrades, however sharp the tiger's fangs may be, however fierce the storm, we must tame them. The enemy is right there among the rocks, yet we shouldn't simply rush straight at them. We must analyse the enemy's position and take it by strategy. Let's think of a way quickly." With Hai-ying still steering, we had a quick discussion meeting, while the rest of us continued rowing. Since I knew nothing about these rocks and shoals I could only listen.

"I think we should avoid the head-on waves," yelled Shui-chu.

"But how can we when the Tiger's Jaws are shaped like this?" Hai-hua yelled back.

"If we avoid the first strong waves and then rush in by sailing along the edge of the current we may make some headway."

"Shui-chu's suggestion sounds reasonable," shouted Hai-ying. "The jaws stand at one end of the reefs; narrow as it is, it's also blocked by the remains of that enemy gunboat. The tide comes in through here and we've come at high-tide which makes going straight against it extremely difficult. But look carefully, comrades. See the peculiar way the waves roll in through the Tiger's Jaws: they're more rapid on the right side and higher. Why? Because of the position of this wreck. Its stern is on the left and its bow on the right, so that the whole skeleton leans outwards. The water swirls around it and creates an undertow. That's why we must rush along the left side if we want to get through."

Under Hai-ying's command, we launched a new attack. Just then, I caught a glimpse of a boat outside the channel. A figure stood erect in the bow, but in a flash, it disappeared from view.

We rushed towards the jaws along the edge of the reefs. This time we were more successful. Rowing was not as strenuous as before. When we were barely ten yards or so from the jaws, we let a particularly large breaker sweep past, then Hai-ying shouted, "Now, comrades, let's get through!" Straining hard, we all worked steadily and although some combers swept across our bows, the sampan edged forward little by little. Just as we entered the narrow jaws, a huge breaker like a small mountain rushed towards us. With a quick twist of the rudder, Hai-ying turned the boat swiftly around the wreck and we all shouted together: **"Be resolute, fear no sacrifice and surmount every difficulty to win victory."** We heard other voices beyond the Tiger's Jaws, shouting these same words in a chorus which soared above the roaring sea. Instantly we gained new strength. We breasted one rolling wave after another as our little craft sliced through the strong current. The old wreck receded rapidly behind our stern. Then, breakers, rocks, rushing current and the whole Tiger-Head Reefs, like a defeated beast, were left far behind us.

The victory was ours!

As soon as our sampan emerged from the jaws, we discovered a large boat moored to a rock on our left. An elderly fisherwoman stood erect in the bow, a pistol in her belt and a fishing line in her hands.

"Hi there, political instructor!" cried Shui-chu at sight of her as our sampan edged alongside.

"How did you know we were coming through the reefs?" asked Hai-ying.

"From a distance we saw that half-way across you turned and went against wind and tide. I guessed immediately where you were heading."

A young girl came closer to us. "Oh, Sister Hai-ying, you and your crew are remarkable," she cried in admiration. "You came through the jaws of the Tiger-Head Reefs in this stormy weather and succeeded in escaping the sea tiger's iron teeth. You've tamed the reefs now."

Nodding towards me Hai-ying told the fisherwoman: "This comrade wanted to come to our island. Since there was no ferry, he came with us."

Only then did the elderly woman turn to me. I, too, was staring at her. When our eyes met, we cried out practically at the same instant. In a flash she leapt over onto our boat. Hands, roughened from decades of rowing, gripped mine tightly. With beating heart, I examined this sturdy woman, a political instructor of the militia guarding our eastern sea. Revolutionary vitality seemed to flow from her and her shrewd eyes, so characteristic of the fisherfolk, shone with discernment. Her short greying hair fluttered in the wind; she looked astute and experienced. Fine wrinkles round her eyes and across her forehead only enhanced the indomitable character of this veteran who had weathered many storms. It seemed to me, she was even more vital than twenty years ago.

"Ah, comrade," she remarked. "Everything's changed. . . ."

"Yes, so it has!" I answered, gazing around me. "Changed indeed. The sea's changed and the women of these sea isles even more so." Then I asked with concern, "Is old uncle still alive and well?"

"You mean Uncle Ming-hai? He's going on seventy but still able to steer a boat to the outer seas," she answered. Then, turning to Hai-ying beside her, she asked, "Look, who's this? Ha, I'm sure you don't recognize her. She's that baby I carried on my back. The child's grown up."

I gazed again on this young commander of the militia exercise I'd shared at sea and said with deep feelings, "Yes, indeed! She certainly has grown up."

The gale increased in intensity and the waves rolled higher. Soon, sails were hoisted on both craft and, riding with the wind, they shot towards Langkangyu across the foam-tipped waves like two stormy petrels skimming over the sea.

The militia women, carrying their rifles, stood bravely and gallantly erect in spite of the tossing sea. Morning sunlight pierced the heavy clouds. It turned the foam golden as it danced over the crests of the waves. The whole eastern sea and the militia women were tinged with crimson.

Suddenly, as our boats sliced through giant breakers, they crashed over the decks and spray showered down on us like sparks from fireworks on festival nights. The girls were drenched with spray. As it showered on the fresh young face of Hai-ying, I remembered what Comrade Ah-chu said more than twenty years before: "We grew up on the salt waves of these island seas."

Illustrated by Tung Chen-sheng

A Shoulder Pole

Yueh Chang-kuei

I had been assigned a job in Green Hills Store deep in the mountains. With my letter of introduction from the county department of commerce, I went to take up my new post. As I arrived at the store gate, I heard a beautiful voice singing with bell-like clarity in the courtyard:

> I peddle my wares uphill and down,
> My shoulder pole links countryside and town.

Entering the gate, I saw a girl in a straw hat squatting in the centre of the courtyard and skilfully repairing a shoulder pole. She stopped singing at my approach and jumped to her feet, pushing back the straw hat to reveal two short, thick braids. She looked twenty or so, not tall but well built with big, slightly slanting eyes. She laid down her tool and hurried towards me.

"If I'm not mistaken, you must be Comrade Chang Yen-chun, our new colleague," she said with sparkling eyes.

"And you?. . ."

"I am Shan Li-ying."

Shan Li-ying? Why, then, I'd be working under her! They had told me in the county that Shan Li-ying, in charge of Green Hills Store, was a very fine comrade. I ought to learn from her. I had imagined her to be an experienced middle-aged woman. However, she was little more than a girl.

"What job will you be giving me?" I asked bluntly.

"Do you want to start work at once? Why not have a rest?"

She narrowed her eyes as if to size me up. Then, without waiting for my answer, she led me to the backyard of the store. There, neatly laid out, were four baskets with two shoulder poles. Two baskets were filled with farm tools, the others with daily necessities. I glanced at her in bewilderment and found that she was regarding me with smiling eyes. From her expression I guessed what she had in mind.

"Is this my job?" I asked. She nodded. I was startled. In the letter of introduction still in my pocket, it was very clearly stated that I was to be a "sales clerk." That meant serving behind the counter. But now it seemed I was to carry these heavy baskets. I stared at the young manager who was about my own age. Before I could speak she picked up a pole and solemnly handed it to me.

"There. This is yours."

I had a look at it. *Aiya*! It was an old pole with some parts so worn that they shone. The two ends, having split, had been bound with wire. In the act of reaching out, I drew back my hands.

Seeing my hesitation, she knit her brows. "Well? Don't you like the idea?" I could only stare at her dumbfounded. She looked at the pole, then at me. "Yen-chun," she said seriously, "there's more to this pole than meets the eye. It stands for the glorious tradition of our Green Hills Store!"

I couldn't understand why she was so worked up. Taking the pole, I found that it had the characters "Serve the People" carved on the back. This had been done recently by the look of it. Those three words warmed my heart. Grasping the pole, I lifted the heavy load. Little Shan's face lit up. Watching me with narrowed eyes she burst into laughter, laughter crystal-clear as a mountain spring cascading down a cliff.

*

The winding track was steep and stony. Climbing just one hill with my load made the sweat pour down my back. Breathless, choking and hot, I longed to take a rest. Several times I nearly put down my baskets. But Little Shan carrying a heavier load than I swung steadily along, her head high, her braids swinging at each step. And as she walked she sang.

Soon our path dipped to wind through a valley. We saw a young man coming towards us. He was in a hurry, no doubt on urgent business.

"Hullo, Young Ma! What's all the hurry?" Little Shan called.

"I'm going to town," he replied without raising his head.

"Oh! Everybody's busy now, each one doing the work of two. But you have time to potter about in town."

"Unless on business, I never go to town, not even if you'd carry me in a sedan-chair."

"What's your business today?" Little Shan asked.

"It's no use my telling you!" Young Ma replied with a wave of his hand. He started to leave but the girl with her two baskets blocked the way. "What way is that to talk?" she demanded. "If you don't tell me, I won't let you pass. Are you going to the Farm Tools Plant?"

"How did you know?" The young man was astonished.

"I guessed," she laughed, raising her head. "Are you going to buy spare parts for your weeders?"

"Who told you that?" Young Ma was mystified.

"Never you mind." She brushed his question aside. "How many machines are out of order? And what parts do you want?"

"How many? Don't you know?" He winked.

"Of course I know." She reckoned with her fingers. "There are eighteen weeders in all in your brigade. Four of them are out of order. Three have broken teeth and one has a broken axle. Am I right?"

The young man was stunned. "Absolutely right! How did you know?"

"How can we develop the economy and ensure supplies if we don't know the situation?" Little Shan smoothed back her hair, then took a heavy cardboard box from one of her baskets and gave it to the young man. "Here's what you want to buy."

Stepping forward I noticed that on the box was written: New Lane Brigade, three sets of weeder teeth and one axle.

The young man was so pleased as he took the box that he didn't know what to say. All of a sudden, however, he put it down and grabbed the pole from Little Shan.

"Let me carry this for you."

"No! We are not going the same way," she objected.

"Aren't you going to Golden Bay? I'm going back to the brigade now. Let's go together."

Picking up her load, Little Shan pointed to a ridge which zigzagged through the fields. "We'll go this way," she declared.

"What's the idea?" asked the young man. "Why not go by the path?"

Little Shan gave him a shove. "All right, go and get on with your work. We don't need you to be our guide."

I realized that the girl must have some reason for this change of route. Before I could ask her what it was she said: "We can take a look at the crops if we go this way. Do some investigation. Don't we say: No investigation, no right to speak?"

"There is nothing to investigate here," I said without thinking. "Our job is to sell the goods we have in stock."

"What's that?. . ." Turning around, she asked in a serious voice: "Do you know why I gave you that pole?" I shook my head. "The people of the whole country are learning from Tachai," she went on. "Should we carry our goods to the countryside and try to help the poor and lower-middle peasants? Or should we sit waiting for them to come to our store? This is a basic question in commercial work. How best can we serve the people?" Thereupon, she told me a story.

Last spring, the production teams had decided to rebuild their pigsties in order to collect more manure. On hearing this, she thought they would need cement. Thereupon, sitting in her office, she made a plan to lay in a stock of cement and bought twenty tons from town. But a whole week passed. Nobody came to buy cement. She was puzzled. So she went down to the different teams and found that they had rebuilt the pigsties with stone, without using any cement, as a result of learning from Tachai's revolutionary style of self-reliance.

"Subjectiveness landed me in trouble!" said Little Shan with heartfelt feeling. "It's not enough to want to serve the people. You must make thorough investigations too. Otherwise you can't do your work well."

We talked as we walked and had soon covered several miles. Suddenly Little Shan halted. "Look! Why have those young paddy plants turned yellow?" she cried, pointing to the paddy fields. I saw that all the young plants were a lush green except for one patch so small that one had to look carefully to spot it. "Maybe it lacks fertilizer," I said without consideration.

"Don't say maybe. Hit-or-miss methods won't do." She glanced at me. Taking her shoes off, she waded into the muddy fields. Bending over, she pulled up a young plant and showed it to me. "Comrade Yen-chun, do you know what's wrong with it?" I examined it and found that both stem and root were still sound. Only the tip of the shoot was a bit yellow as if it had been scorched.

"This is the first time we've grown paddy here," she said anxiously, knitting her brows. "We have no experience. If we can't clear this up at once it will soon spread. It will not only influence this year's harvest but also influence the popularization of paddy growing in our mountainous area." On hearing this, I was also very worried. "What shall we do?" I asked. Little Shan kept silent but her black eyes flashed as she again waded into the paddy fields and scooped up some mud. "You go to Golden

Bay first with your goods," she instructed me. "I'm going to the agro-technical station."

I looked up at the sky. It had darkened. Black rain-clouds were converging from all sides. The summit of the mountain was already shrouded in mist. Any moment the storm might break. "Why not wait until after the storm, Little Shan," I advised.

"A storm is nothing. Disease prevention is like putting out a fire. We can't delay for one minute." So saying, she shouldered her pole and hurried off. After a few steps, however, she stopped and turned back to offer me a green raincoat.

"The cover on that back basket of yours leaks. Put my raincoat over it," she cried.

"How about you?"

"It's the goods that matter. . . ." The rest of the sentence was drowned by a peal of thunder.

*

Approaching Golden Bay Village, I saw some villagers discussing something as they sheltered from the rain. When they found that I was a new saleswoman, they wanted to know where Little Shan was. Before I could open my mouth a young fellow bellowed: "Have you brought insecticide for our paddy?" I noticed that they also had some young plants in their hands. "I don't know what's wrong with the paddy. How could I bring insecticide?" I answered.

"Little Shan is not like you," retorted the young fellow. The old brigade leader shot a glance at him. "Don't lose your temper. You must take these young plants to the agro-technical station at once."

"Little Shan has already taken some there," I put in, before the young fellow could leave.

"She has, has she?" The old brigade leader beamed. Looking up at the sky, he took off his raincoat and put it over the youngster's arm. "Quick! Go and meet her." The young fellow promptly dashed off through the pouring rain.

At that moment, my pole caught the old brigade leader's eye.

"That pole!. . ." he exclaimed. Walking up to me, he gripped the pole. He examined it from one end to the other, turning it over and over.

"What do you see in this pole, brigade leader?" I laughed. "It has no flowers on it. What's so special about it?"

"It has no flowers on it. But it's steeped in the blood of our old store-keeper."

"The blood of your old store-keeper?"

Looking up at the distant mountain wrapped in mist, he told me the shoulder pole's story:

"Before liberation, the poor and lower-middle peasants in this area had to walk for scores of miles if they wanted to buy something. Profiteers seized this chance to speculate in goods. We had to give them a pound of medicinal herbs in exchange for a box of matches. A pelt purchased only a pound of kerosene. How cruel those blood-suckers were!

"Soon after liberation, the local people's government opened this Green Hills Store here. At first, the store was small, run by just one comrade. That was the old store-keeper. It was he who, shouldering this selfsame pole, brought us Chairman Mao's concern for the poor and lower-middle peasants. At the same time, with this pole, he carried our love for our socialist motherland to the folk on the plain. Everybody called this store "the shoulder-pole store." But a handful of class enemies hated it. Early one morning, the old store-keeper was carrying goods to the villagers along a mountain path when two ruffians rushed out from the forest with clubs and knives in their hands. Like savage wolves they barred the old store-keeper's way. In a rage, the old store-keeper shouted: "You can kill me. But you can't block this path!" Raising the pole he charged the enemy. Our old store-keeper fought to the last drop of his blood for the interests of the people."

"What was his name?" I inquired with feeling.

"Shan Ju-sung. He was Shan Li-ying's father."

"Ah! Little Shan's father!" I exclaimed. Taking the pole, I clasped it to my chest. I could find no words for all I wanted to say. By giving me this pole with such a glorious history, Little Shan had shown great faith in me. She had also shown how much she expected of me. But I. . . . My eyes filled with tears. I looked at the steep path shaded by green pines. This path seemed a cord which nothing could snap, running from the foot to the summit of the mountain.

"It was the old store-keeper who trod out this path," the old brigade leader told me meaningly.

Yes! Acting on Chairman Mao's instruction, **"Develop the economy and ensure supplies,"** this revolutionary predecessor of ours had blazed this rugged trail with his firm steps. Little Shan had inherited her father's pole, had shouldered a heavy revolutionary burden and was striding boldly forward. Now the pole was on my shoulder. I determined to follow in the old store-keeper's footsteps along the path. I would follow it to the end. . . .

The rain stopped. The whole sky looked like a broad lake, with scattered clouds like small boats drifting across the lake. The green hills and trees and the red flowers were doubly fresh and beautiful, newly washed by the rain. A gentle breeze blew over the mountains. We heard a voice singing with bell-like clarity, a voice familiar and dear to all of us.

"Little Shan has come back!" The old brigade leader ran to meet her.

The sun appeared again. A rainbow arched over the sky like a splendid, many-coloured bridge spanning high mountain peaks. Under the rainbow, on the winding path, appeared the short, sturdy figure of Little Shan. From her shoulder pole hung two baskets loaded with farm tools and insecticides. Each step she took was firm and forceful. The golden sunlight mantled her whole form, and beneath her feet stretched the long unbroken path.

Illustrated by Chou Chien-fu

When the Persimmons Ripened

Ko Niu

Like a torch, the autumn wind turned the trees in the valley and over the hilltops a bright crimson until the whole mountain seemed aflame. Under a deep azure sky, the undulating ranges were a lovely sight.

A persimmon tree at the bottom of the gully looked like a huge red sunshade from a distance. Now and again, scarlet leaves fluttered down from the branches, rustling as they reached the ground. Suddenly a ripe persimmon fell with a plop on the tent below the tree, rolled slowly to one edge and dropped by its door-flap.

Young Chin poked his head out at the sound. What a pity, he thought, at sight of the bruised persimmon.

Modelling his actions on his squad leader's, he picked up the ripe fruit and wiped it with his towel. A delicious aroma tickled the young fighter's nostrils. Chin seemed to see Li Min, the squad leader, his full lips pursed in concentration as he stooped to pick up fallen fruit. Those big hands, calloused from handling rough stones, could swing a heavy hammer as if it were a stem of flax but lifted each persimmon as though it weighed a ton. At such times Li always untied his towel and cleaned the fruit, humming under his breath the song about the people's army's discipline.

The whole squad was out at work. Young Chin, whose turn it was to do the cooking, was the only one in the camp. As the song rang in his ears, he recalled their arrival in the gully a couple of months ago.

*

The squad had come here early in July on an assignment connected with preparedness against war. No sooner had they put down their kit than they discovered that there was no space in the gully for them to set up a tent. The whole valley was planted with young maize. Craggy cliffs rose precipitously on both sides and further down was a swift-running stream. There was simply no room to pitch camp.

One or two comrades proposed putting up their tent in the maize field — they need only take up twenty square metres at the most. In his eagerness to get cracking, Chin shook Li's broad shoulders, urging him to report back at once to the company. Li, however, remained impassive, his eyes sweeping the valley. Suddenly his eyebrows twitched. Pointing a finger he exclaimed, "Isn't that a good place to camp?" The men saw a mound in the middle of the maize field surmounted by a big persimmon tree. With the squad at his heels, Li strode to the tree and began pacing out the ground underneath.

At last he pronounced, "It's just big enough, we'll set up our tent against the tree. There are paths on both sides, so that's fine."

"Of course it's better not to encroach on farmland, but the ground here is so uneven, we'll need at least three days to level it." Chin was anxious to waste no time in pitching camp.

Li gathered the men round him under the persimmon tree. Together they studied Chairman Mao's directive, **"The army must become one with the people so that they see it as their own army. Such an army will be invincible."** This teaching warmed the men's hearts. Then Li told them an anecdote.

Twenty-three years before this, when our army was fighting to liberate a city, a detachment of the People's Liberation Army had infiltrated the place late one winter night. In order not to disturb the inhabitants, the men unpacked their kit and spent the night out in the streets. The people's army's first concern is the people. Hearts ablaze with love, they disregarded the cold. When an old woman opened her door early the next morning, what she saw took her breath away. There was a layer of frost on the men's light covering. The old woman's eyes grew misty. What fine soldiers these were! They would shed their own blood in the fighting to protect the people's lives and property. Now that the city was liberated, they were content to sleep in the streets.... She hurriedly woke her husband and together they roused the neighbourhood.

With such devotion to the cause, our revolutionary predecessors won city after city, village after village, till the whole of China was liberated....

This story had first been told by the old battalion commander. Although the men had heard it a dozen times they were especially moved by it today. Li himself was deeply stirred.

"Comrades, have you ever reflected how pregnant in meaning it is, the name PLA? The people's own army! How much those few words signify!" His eyes swept the men around him before he asked: "Well, how shall we pitch camp?"

The squad leader's words fell on Chin's ears like timely rain on a thirsty field. They helped his understanding to grow apace. After rolling up his sleeves he shook Li's shoulders again. "Let's get started!" he cried. "If we can't set up our tent by nightfall, we'll sleep out under the tree."

The whole squad set to at once with spade and pick.

All this the local poor and lower-middle peasants observed with approval. Old Uncle Hsing-fu, his heart turbulent with emotion, stroked his silvery beard and voiced his appreciation. Then at a signal from him, many peasants with hoes and rakes joined the men at work. Soldiers and peasants together levelled the ground under the tree in no time at all. Without pausing even to mop his perspiring forehead, Li inspected the surrounding maize field with Chin, bending low to make sure that not even a small clod of earth was pressing down upon the growing plants.

When pink sunset clouds melted into darkness in the western sky, the rousing strains of *The Three Main Rules of Discipline and the Eight Points for Attention* rang out from the tent under the tree. The squad leader started the song, singing lustily:

> Revolutionary soldiers must always remember,
> The three rules and eight points. . . .

*

"Is our meal ready, Chin?"

Li's voice broke into Chin's train of memories. The men were back from work, marching behind Li whose sturdy frame had already appeared on the mound. His uniform was almost white with much washing but the tabs on his collar were still a vivid red. Chin went up to him and said, "Look at this persimmon, squad leader."

"What a pity!" Li's face clouded as he took the fruit. "Another one so badly bruised." Wiping the persimmon on the hem of his tunic, he stepped into the tent and placed it in a basin. "This is the nineteenth," he muttered half to Chin and half to himself.

The small square levelled by the men in front of the tent was well shaded by the tree. Peasants passing by often stopped to chat with the men off duty here. It was also a place of amusement for the men after their meal. There were countless persimmon and date trees in these mountain gullies but there was something unusual about this one. The thick trunk was heavily scored by a conspicuous six-inch scar made by a knife. The bark had grown over the cut after many years, but the traces of the gash would always be visible. Half hidden by the thick foliage hung luscious persimmons in clusters of twos and threes. The fruit was exceptionally large and plump. But although it was quite late in the autumn, the owner of the tree had not yet turned up to pick it. Why was that? This was a question which puzzled all the men.

"Perhaps the peasants are too busy harvesting their crops. They can't spare the time to pick fruit." This was Chin's guess.

"But what a pity to let so many persimmons fall and get bruised like that."

"We must put a stop to this somehow."

All agreed on this point and turned to the squad leader.

Li had heard Uncle Hsing-fu say something about leaving these persimmons for the PLA comrades to enjoy. That would never do. The persimmons should be picked of course, no matter by whom. They couldn't just be left on the tree like that.

"I know what," he said with a decisive gesture. "We'll pick all the persimmons now and, when we've found out who the owner is, we can deliver the fruit to him. How's that?"

"That's an idea." Chin blinked. "But what if we can't discover who the owner is?"

"Don't worry, I'll find a way," said Li. But in his heart he was also a little worried.

Now that the squad leader had given the order, some of the men climbed the tree while others worked under it. Before long, six large crates were filled with persimmons. The crates were well lined with old newspapers and Li himself placed the nineteen windfalls with the other fruit, handling them gingerly as though they were eggs.

When this job was finished Chin beamed. Indeed all the men felt easier in their minds now, for every time a persimmon fell it had distressed them.

From his experience of several years in the army, Li realized that it would be no easy task to discover the owner of the persimmons. Even if they succeeded in finding out, it would still be difficult to deliver the fruit. A week went by and they were no nearer the solution of their problem. Soon it was Sunday again. Li sent men out in two directions to join the villagers at work so that while farming together they might find some clue to the owner of the tree.

By noon both groups had returned. Instead of finding out the required information, they themselves had nearly been "caught" by the peasants who insisted on thrusting dried dates and ripe persimmons into their hands. When they declined these the old people looked offended. "Who asked you to fetch water and do other jobs for us?" they demanded. "So you refuse to eat our fruit, eh? Well, if that's the way you feel you'd better stop coming."

When the PLA men mentioned the persimmon tree on the mound all the villagers, old and young alike, knew about it and spoke of it with pride and affection. But when asked whom the fruit belonged to, the peasants stalled. "Why, who bothers to lay claim to a few persimmons?"

The more generous the peasants were, the more eager the PLA men were to find the fruit's owner. Li urged the squad to search for more "clues." Suddenly Chin clapped his forehead. "Why didn't it occur to us before? Trees go with the land they're on, and this land belongs to Team Two. That surely means the persimmons belong to that team." The others were convinced by this reasoning. And Li had heard Uncle Hsing-fu say that the mound was the watershed dividing the land of Teams Two and Three. That being the case, the persimmon tree must belong to one or the other of the two teams. It was decided that after their meal they'd take the persimmons to their owner.

A golden sun in a deep blue sky shed a mellow glow over the mountain path as marching down from the persimmon tree came men carrying six large crates, sounding gongs and beating a drum. At their head was squad leader Li Min.

When the company's political instructor visited their tent the previous evening, Li Min had told him about the case of the persimmons. The instructor had looked appreciatively from the surrounding mountain peaks to the eager young fighters by his side. He had commended them for what they had done. The men now swung along vigorously and soon arrived at Team Two. The team leader was taken by surprise but a second glance told him why the soldiers were there. When Li started to explain their mission, he cut in:

"You've made a mistake, squad leader. These persimmons aren't ours. You've come to the wrong place."

Li Min was prepared for that. "No mistake, comrade." The men also chimed in, citing as their reason the custom for the ownership of trees to go with that of the land.

The team leader was taken aback for a moment. "The tree really belongs to Team Three," he said presently. "But if I were you I'd keep the persimmons because it's no use your trying to send them back."

The men had no alternative but to turn round, gongs, drum and all, and head for Team Three.

To their surprise the leader of Team Three, a woman, also refused the fruit. She fobbed them off with exactly the same reply as had the leader of Team Two, concluding, "Keep the persimmons for yourselves. Lugging them around is only a waste of time."

Only then did it dawn on the men that the two teams were in cahoots. Li Min frowned thoughtfully. He would not admit defeat, but they had gone from one team to another with gongs and drum, talking till they were hoarse, and the six crates of persimmons were still on their hands. The problem seemed even more complicated now. He decided to enlist the support of Uncle Hsing-fu who, as an ex-guerrilla, would surely help them out. Unfortunately the old man was away at a meeting in the commune. All Li could do was direct his men to carry the persimmons back to camp.

That night the squad sat around the hurricane-lamp to re-study *"The Three Main Rules of Discipline and the Eight Points for Attention"* laid down by Chairman Mao. Inspired by the examples of veteran revolutionaries in implementing the rules of discipline, the men were all the more determined to find out the owner of the persimmons.

Uncle Hsing-fu arrived at noon the next day with his little grandson. The men went out of the tent to welcome him, then clustered round him under the tree. Li sensed that the two production teams had sent him.

"I suppose you know what happened yesterday, uncle." He broached the subject without further preliminaries.

The old man laughed jovially. "Yes, I've heard." He lit his pipe. After a few puffs he said, "Well, I'll be quite frank. This tree stands on the boundary line between two teams and it has never been quite clear which team should pick the fruit. Your coming this year was a stroke of good luck for us. The poor and lower-middle peasants of both teams are of one mind. Neither team will pick the persimmons this year, but let the PLA comrades enjoy the ripe fruit. Since the villagers want to make you a gift, you must accept the fruit."

So that explained everything! Chin said with feeling, "Uncle, we fully appreciate the poor and lower-middle peasants' generosity, but naturally we can't accept the gift. Chairman Mao teaches us not to take a single needle or thread from the masses...."

Before the old man could say anything, his little grandson piped up: "But, uncle, these are persimmons, not needle or thread."

This remark set the men laughing. Li hugged the child. "At any rate, we can't take the persimmons. If we must take them, we will pay for them out of our own pockets."

Uncle Hsing-fu stuck to his point. "You've got to keep the fruit. You PLA comrades work wholeheartedly for the people, what's wrong with your eating a few persimmons?" He stood up and gave the tree a loving glance before continuing, "Did you know that Eighth Route Army men shed their blood under this tree?" The men stared as he stroked the scar on the trunk. Lighting his pipe again, the old man launched into his tale:

Many years ago just at this season when the persimmons were ripe, the dogs outside the village started barking early one morning. The White brigands were coming. Thirty Kuomintang troops had surrounded the village. Smoke rose as fires broke out and the villagers, caught off guard, had no time to hide and were rounded up together under this persimmon tree. Broken branches hung dangling from shreds of bark. Half-eaten fruit littered the ground. The bandits levelling their guns at the peasants ordered them to lead the way to the Eighth Route Army's hide-outs. Gritting their teeth, the villagers refused. They would not lift a finger to help the reactionaries against their own army. When no one would stir a step, the officer in charge unsheathed his sword. With a wild slash at the persimmon tree he shouted, "Take us to the Eighth Route!" Not a single person moved. In a rage, the officer ordered the soldiers to load their guns. They were all set to mow the villagers down. Dozens of lives were at stake.

"Do you want to live or die?" howled the officer.

The peasants' eyes blazed, their blood boiled. Signalling to each other with their eyes, they decided to have it out with the bandits. They mustn't wait to be slaughtered. They would fight.

Suddenly, a dozen or so Eighth Route Army men led by platoon leader Big Chiang rushed down from the mountain. Sharp bayonets mounted on their rifles, they charged the bandits. Before the officer could pull out his gun, Big Chiang put a bullet through him. All this happened so fast that the bandits didn't know which way to turn. They milled round in panic. The villagers, emboldened by the coming of their own troops, pounced on the enemy. A bitter clash ensued.

People and armymen fighting together soon routed the bandits. But Big Chiang gave his life in the struggle. His blood spattered the persimmon tree.

After that the village's young men joined the Eighth Route Army while those left behind organized a guerrilla detachment. Uncle Hsing-fu was the guerrilla leader. Shoulder to shoulder, peasants and soldiers patrolled the village. Together they practised target shooting and together they took aim at the enemy. Fighting for liberation and heading for the same goal, army and people were bound by strong feelings of kinship.

Uncle Hsing-fu eyed the big tree which had weathered so many storms. "It's very strange," he continued. "This tree has grown more luxuriantly ever since and its fruit seems larger and redder than before. The villagers say it's drawn strength from the martyr's blood."

After a pause the old man continued, "Every year when the fruit turns red, the poor and lower-middle peasants think of Big Chiang and of our armymen.

Now that at last you are here, how can you refuse to accept the persimmons?"

This tale touched the men's heart-strings. The glowing persimmons symbolized the fervent love of the people. How could they still say no?

Li Min turned to whisper with the men, then to Uncle Hsing-fu he said, "We'll accept the persimmons and never forget what the poor and lower-middle peasants expect of us. We shall learn from the revolutionary spirit of Big Chiang and safeguard our fruits of victory. As a token of gratitude we. . . ."

Before he could finish, Chin emerged from the tent and handed Uncle Hsing-fu a large red envelope. In it there were a letter from the soldiers expressing their thanks for the peasants' loving concern and the money for the persimmons.

Uncle Hsing-fu, his mission fulfilled, started home with his grandson, farewelled by drumming and gonging. On the thick trunk of the tree was pasted a piece of red paper with the words written by Li Min: "Carry the revolutionary tradition forward, win still greater glory."

Then came the order to strike camp. Li Min and his comrades decided to present the persimmons to the Third Company of the militia which was working on the construction site with them. They started out with the crates of fruit, marching down the mountain path trodden years before them by the Eighth Route Army.

Rounding a turn in the road, the squad disappeared from sight but the song embodying the love between army and people reverberated through the valley:

> Revolutionary discipline in mind,
> The people's fighters always love the people.
> Guarding our land, we march for ever forward,
> Supported by the people wherever we go.

Illustrated by Kang Tung

Home Leave

Hsueh Chiang

Some time ago Political Commissar Wang Chiang went to a company of his regiment to size up the situation there. Finding that Company Commander Liu's wife had volunteered to work in a mountain district and would be setting off soon for her new post, he immediately granted Liu home leave to go back to his village and see his wife off.

As Liu was on the point of leaving, he heard that Squad Leader Kao Wu's mother was ill. But Kao when questioned declared it a false alarm. His squad had an important task still to finish.

Liu knew from years of experience in the army that where personal affairs are concerned soldiers will never admit to having any problems. He suspected that Kao was holding something back. Just then, however, regimental headquarters rang up again urging him to delay no longer. So having delegated his work to others, he slung his kit-bag with an embroidered red star over his shoulder and lost no further time in setting off.

As the red bus bowled along the smooth highway, Liu could not get Kao Wu's mother off his mind. He decided to break his journey to call at the squad leader's home. And as soon as the bus had passed Mount Taliang, Kao's village came in sight.

Liu alighted and headed straight for the west end of the village, to stop before a new house with a tiled roof. Two red plaques on the door indicated that a soldier from this family had died for the revolution, and that one of its members was now serving in the army.

"Are you at home, aunt?" he called.

The woman who came to the door was younger than Liu had expected.

"Aunt Kao is ill," she explained, inviting him in.

Liu found Aunt Kao lying on the bed.

Opening her eyes with an effort, Aunt Kao thought for a moment that it was her own son standing there before her. What a happy surprise! But then, her vision clearing, she saw that this PLA man was taller than her son and broader in the face. His big eyes under thick black eyebrows were bright with concern.

"I'm Liu Cheng, Aunt Kao, your son's comrade-in-arms," said the company commander by way of introduction. "I heard you were unwell, that's why

I've come." He sat down on the bed beside the old woman.

"Some time ago we had a spell of rain," said Aunt Kao's neighbour. "Aunt Kao caught a chill while out collecting green stuff for our brigade's pigs. That brought on bilious attacks, and she had to take to her bed. Our brigade cadres wanted to send a message to your company asking for leave for young Kao, but she wouldn't hear of it...."

Liu was too moved to reply immediately. The sight of the old woman ill in bed and the thought of spirited young Kao convinced him that he had done the right thing by coming here.

"You must have had your hands full nursing Aunt Kao," he said to the neighbour. "This is a busy farming season, too. Let me take over now and look after her." He saw the neighbour off, then came back inside.

"You know the old saying, aunt," he said. " 'Even a strong man needs food.' Hot noodles with hot soup are just the thing to settle your stomach, I'm sure." With that he rolled up his sleeves and, ignoring Aunt Kao's attempts to stop him, started mixing dough.

Liu happened to be an old hand at making noodles. As he kneaded the dough he described the good progress young Kao had made since joining the army. Aunt Kao listened and watched him, fascinated, until suddenly something distracted her attention. She propped herself up to reach out for Liu's worn kit-bag which he had laid on the bed. And as she examined the red star embroidered on the bag, her lips twitched.

"What is it?" asked Liu with concern. His inquiry aroused Aunt Kao from her reveries, but did nothing to solve the question in her mind.

"Was this kit-bag issued to you by your company?" she ventured.

"There's a story behind that, aunt." Liu wiped his hands, sat down on the edge of the bed and embarked on an explanation.

"One pitch-black night during the War to Resist U.S. Aggression and Aid Korea, the rain started coming down in torrents. Our company's mission was to attack a height north of Sikyundong; but a big river barred the way, both its banks under enemy fire. Our old commander took up a position on the north bank to direct our company across in safety. Then flashes flared up on the south bank, and shells started exploding all round us. One of our men, Wang Chiang, was just communicating with headquarters when our company commander sprang forward to push him to the ground and cover him with his own body. The next moment shrapnel ripped through this kit-bag and wounded our commander. Comrade Wang Chiang came through unhurt, and passed on headquarters' instruction to our unit; but our commander — we all thought the world of him — died a hero's death. That's why this kit-bag of his with the embroidered red star is now one of our company's most treasured heirlooms. It reminds us of our revolutionary tradition, inspiring us to learn from those before us who so bravely laid down their lives."

Liu had hardly finished his story when Aunt Kao asked anxiously: "What was your company commander's name?"

"Kao Chan-feng."

"I thought as much!" Holding the kit-bag in both hands, Aunt Kao examined it closely under the lamp. The red star which she had embroidered at night, just before her husband left for Korea, seemed brighter than ever before.

"Did you know Kao Chan-feng, aunt?" asked the company commander.

"He was my husband. My boy's father."

Liu stared in amazement at the kit-bag, now even more precious in his eyes. Young Kao Wu had never breathed a word about this.

"I've been wondering all these years what became of this kit-bag," continued Aunt Kao. "Just fancy your turning up with it today! . . . But how did it come into your hands?"

"As to that . . . I've done nothing really to deserve it." The company commander made haste to change the subject. "I must see about boiling these noodles."

Soon water was bubbling in the pan. When Liu raised the lid, steam eddied out. The whole room seemed warmer.

After two days of nursing Aunt Kao was better, but she was not yet fully recovered. After preparing her breakfast on the third day, Liu went into the courtyard to chop firewood. Suddenly he heard retching inside. He ran in and found Aunt Kao vomiting again. Liu decided to fetch the commune doctor, then ring up company headquarters to send Kao Wu home to look after his mother. He hurried to the commune health centre, only to find a notice pinned to the wall: "On our rounds to the Hohsi Brigade this morning. Out-patients will please come this afternoon."

Company Commander Liu began to feel worried. He dashed to the post office and rang up his unit, then set off at full speed to the Hohsi Brigade on the other side of the river to fetch a doctor. Dark clouds were gathering in the sky. The growl of thunder heralded a storm.

The stream flowing down the valley looked like a sharp sword cutting the hills into two. By the time Liu reached the bank, rain was pelting down. Wiping his streaming face, he strained his eyes towards the village hazily visible on the other side, wishing there were some way to vault across. The roaring torrent and driving rain reminded him of that battle in Korea during which his old company commander Kao Chan-feng had given his own life to save a comrade. A force much greater than himself spurred him forward. Storm or no storm, he must ford the stream at once.

After the doctor fetched by Liu had examined Aunt Kao, he gave Liu a package of herbs. "These will cure the patient in no time," he predicted.

This reassurance took a load off Liu's mind and banished his fatigue. Squatting down by the stove, he started to brew the medicine.

Aunt Kao's illness took a marked turn for the better after she drank the medicine. The next day, she hung the old kit-bag over Liu's shoulder and urged him to be off. She had learned the previous evening that Liu had obtained home leave to see his wife, and she would not hear of him staying a single day longer.

"You're not completely better yet, aunt," he protested. "Let me stay at least until young Kao comes back."

"No, I'm quite well enough now to look after myself," she answered.

Since she was adamant, Liu did not insist. But there were many things he had not got round to doing for Aunt Kao. Sitting down on the bed, he took out his pen and wrote on a slip of paper for young Kao all the chores he thought still needed doing.

"Hurry, or you'll miss the bus," urged Aunt Kao. She saw Liu to the gate, and stood there watching until he was out of sight.

The sounding of a horn announced the approach of the bus. It entered the village just as Liu reached the bus stop.

"Company Commander!" called a familiar voice, and from the bus down jumped a beaming young soldier.

"So you've come, Kao Wu." Liu grasped both Kao's hands in his own. "Your mother's much better now. Hurry up home and take good care of her."

The young soldier gripped his commander's hands, not knowing how to express his gratitude.

As the setting sun reddened the distant horizon, Liu climbed aboard the bus and it started off. Sitting quietly by a window, he thought over the happenings of the last few days. Clearly etched in his mind's eye was the kindly face of old Aunt Kao, wife of his former company commander and mother of one of his men.

Illustrated by Huang Chia-yu

彩色的田野

*

外文出版社出版(北京)
1973年(34开)第一版
编号:(英)10050—762
00070
10—E—1308P

This book sho
the Library on or
stamped below.

A fine of ten cer
by retaining it be
time.

Please return pr